The Best Medicine

Cardiff Libraries
www.cardiff.gov.uk/libraries

Llyfrgelloedd Caerdydd
www.caerdydd.gov.uk/llyfrgelloedd

The Best Medicine

First published in 2016 by
Little Island Books
7 Kenilworth Park
Dublin 6W
Ireland

ISBN: 978-1-910411-51-3

A British Library Cataloguing in Publication record for this book is available from the British Library.

Insides designed and typeset by redrattledesign.com
Cover design by The Project Twins

Printed in Poland by Drukarnia Skleniarz

Little Island receives financial assistance from
The Arts Council/An Chomhairle Ealaíon and the Arts Council of Northern Ireland

10 9 8 7 6 5 4 3 2 1

The Best Medicine

Christine Hamill

Little
Island

Acknowledgements

The author and publisher are delighted to thank the comedian Harry Hill for allowing us to include him in this novel. Of course, the Harry Hill here is fictional – the narrator's *idea* of him – but we reckon the real Harry Hill is every bit as great.

For Callan

1

Yeti Another Bad Thing

The bad things started happening one at a time.

At first I hardly noticed. It was just small stuff like Mum buying the wrong cereal – porridge instead of Coco Pops. Then it was the juice – she accidentally bought bottled water instead. Shortly after that she started reading this weird book about how to stay calm which had exercises in it that she made me help her with. I had to ring this tiny tinkly bell every fifteen seconds or so while she stared at the pips on a strawberry and *stilled her inner self*. Strawberry pips are very calming apparently. But not calming enough; after about a week Mum flung her copy of *101 Ways to Stay Calm* across the room at me and said if I didn't stop playing the tune to Harry Hill's TV show on the tinkly bell, she'd have me adopted. But I didn't believe her: everyone loves that tune.

Still, I went and had a lie-down in my room after that and practised Way to Stay Calm No 89. The book said you should not make negative statements such as *I don't like cheese on toast*; you should practice saying what you *do* like. I tried really hard to do that exercise but it was impossible: what's not to like about cheese on toast?

I held on to the book anyway. I thought maybe it would come in handy if the bad stuff kept happening. And I was right, because the very next day, disaster struck.

I was walking down to art class minding my own business when it happened. A yeti had its hands around my throat and was throttling me. I tried really hard to stay calm by thinking of something positive to say, but you try being positive when someone has their great big sausage fingers wrapped round your neck and see how far you get. Actually, I love sausages so I tried saying *I like sausages* but then I started imagining myself eating The Yeti's fingers. (With beans. And chips.) And that had the reverse effect of making me very, very *un*-calm.

Now, before I go any further I want to apologise here and now to yetis everywhere. They get a bad press and I hate to be the one to add to it, but the fact is I am being bullied by a yeti lookalike. Eddie Lyttle.

Eddie Lyttle is this great big fat bully who wears his hair down the front of his face so you can't see his eyes and goes around terrorising normal people who cut their hair because they actually want to see where they are going. If The Yeti wore glasses, like me, he'd appreciate his eyesight more. Anyway never mind that, back to being strangled.

I was very possibly laughing to myself when the attack happened. And no, I'm not some kind of giggling-freak-weirdo type; I'm a comedian. Well, OK, I'm not a comedian yet, but I'm going to be one when I grow up, like Harry Hill (except maybe not bald). So I need to get in lots of practice and I tell myself jokes all the time. Yetis don't like jokes.

They prefer strangling people. I don't even know where The Yeti came from. A stealth bully, that's him. Which is pretty impressive because he is only fourteen and already he is nearly six foot tall and he's about six foot wide as well, so stealth operations are a big deal for him.

'What you laughing at?' he grunted.

Why do bullies always grunt? Is it something they learn in Bully Club?

Rule one: On no account speak clearly so that your victim might understand you and give you what you want. Grunt at all times to prolong the agony.

It's psychological warfare, that's what it is. I considered telling him that his grunting tactic was probably illegal under the terms of the Geneva Convention. But he was squeezing my neck so tightly that my tonsils were in danger of coming out my nostrils, so a history lesson was really out of the question.

'Agh, lugh, aah monchk, bachk,' I said instead, which translated from the original Chokingese means, 'Lunch money's in bag. Take it.'

The Yeti knew exactly what I was saying. He let go of me, plundered my rucksack, shoved my lunch money into his pocket and trudged off, leaving me late for art.

'You are late,' the teacher said.

Have you noticed how teachers are masters of stating the obvious?

'You are making a habit of this, Philip,' Miss Franks said.

'I'm really sorry, Miss,' I said in what should have been my normal voice, but the words came out in this high-pitched squeal, like some kind of high-frequency signal intended to search out dolphins and other marine life. My voice is always doing that these days. And that's when the next bad thing happened: Lucy Wells burst out laughing at me.

Girls' hearing must be on the same frequency as dolphins', because they all heard me and joined in laughing too and pretty soon the whole class was having a laugh at my expense, but it was Lucy Wells's laughter that stung. She is this blonde goddess who inhabits my art class. I know that sounds a bit sappy and I don't want you to go thinking I am some kind of saddo love sick muppet, but you should see her: she is perfection.

She has beautiful hair and beautiful teeth and beautiful eyes and beautiful ears and beautiful hands, even her knuckles are beautiful. And even when she is sniggering at you for being late and getting told off, she has a beautiful laugh.

Oh, yeah, and one other thing: she hates me.

My best friend Ang (weird name, I'll explain later) is the only person who knows about Lucy and me. I told him about her one lunchtime after I thought she'd smiled at me. Turned out she was smiling at the guy behind me, who is a year above me.

'Behind you *and* above you?' Ang laughed. 'That could prove tricky.'

'It's a spatial challenge,' I said.

'A spatial challenge for a spatial boy,' Ang said.

'Aww,' I said, 'you're spatial too.' And we both fell about laughing.

Good times.

'Philip!' Miss Franks said. 'Are you listening to me? You look like you're in a world of your own.'

'Yes. No. I am,' I said. I can be very articulate when I try.

'That's three weeks in a row,' Miss Franks went on. 'I'm sorry, Philip, but I'll have to give you detention again. It's policy.'

'I'm sorry, Miss Franks,' I said. 'I got held up.'

'*Literally*,' I whispered to Ang as I slid on to a seat beside him.

'The Yeti?' he whispered back.

I nodded. 'He ransacked my rucksack.'

'He rucksacked your ransack?'

'No, he sackranked my sugrag.'

'Your sugrag! The big pervert!'

Then we both burst out laughing and we both ended up with detention. Yet another bad thing.

2
Inspector Clueless

It was nearly five o'clock by the time I got home. I was tired, and I was starving on account of The Yeti relieving me of my lunch money, so I was in no mood for Mum's 'School days are the happiest days of your life' lecture – her default position when I get a detention. I really don't think adults should say stuff like that. It could give a kid a very warped view of adult life. Couldn't they at least pretend there's something to look forward to in the sixty-odd years we'll spend *not* being in school. Anyway they should say pre-school days are the best days of your life because you've never even heard of homework or bullies or goddesses.

And, well, I'm not going to lie to you, I felt like finding my old teddy bear Sir Fluffington and hiding under the duvet and inhaling the old days. But I never got the chance because Mum was waiting in the hall when I got home.

She led me into the living room and sat me down in front of a tray of tea and homemade buns. Hang on – tea plus buns plus detention does not compute. And another thing, Mum had this face on like she was going to tell me something really serious, or worse, something really embarrassing. It looked suspiciously like her facts-of-life face. A face I will never forget. Had she forgotten that I already knew? Please no. Anything but the facts of life again.

I stared at the buns. They had exploded over the sides of the bun cases and were black around the edges. Some were iced, presumably covering up a near-cremation. Mum hardly ever bakes. I looked at her, trying to figure out what was going on. She said nothing. She just looked at me in a creepy sort of way, like she was seeing me for the first time ever.

'What's up?' I said, thinking the sooner this started, the sooner it'd be over.

'Nothing's up,' she said.

Well, that wasn't true. Something was definitely up. Mum trying to bake was a dead give-away.

'You're up to something,' I said.

Mum said, 'I can get nothing past you, inspector.'

She sort of laughed it, but her voice was a bit wobbly, like she was going to start singing but wasn't ready. And yes, my mum does often burst into song for no reason, and yes, it is *very* annoying. She opened her mouth to speak again but her voice had gone all squeaky so she stopped.

'You need oiled,' I said. 'You squeak.'

Now, I know that's not the funniest line in the world but Mum is my number one fan and you'd expect your number one fan to laugh at your jokes, no matter how lame they are. Instead, she burst into tears, ran up the stairs and locked herself in the bathroom.

Hang on, we don't have a lock on the bathroom door.

I'm always going on about how I am a growing boy and how I need my privacy and how Mum is an ageing woman and she needs her privacy but she'd never listened. Until now.

I climbed the stairs and stood outside the door. Tried the handle, definitely locked. She'd done it, taken my advice for once and never even told me. I could hear her blowing her nose like she was trying to blow her brains out through her nostrils. I didn't feel right stalking someone on the toilet so I rattled the handle. Just to let her know I was there.

'I'll be out in a minute,' Mum said through a hail of snot. 'Have a bun. They're wholemeal.'

I went back downstairs and picked the icing off one of her buns and tried to think up some fresh jokes to cheer her up.

When Mum came down I noticed her eyes; they were all red and piggy-looking. That's when I knew things were bad. I remember the piggy-eyed look after Dad left.

'What's up?' I said in my best fake-cheerful voice. I thought maybe Dad had come back to upset her and I was already planning how I could trip him up and knock him out and have him disposed of.

'Hay fever,' Mum said and tried to feed me another bun.

Hay fever? Hmm, that was new. I looked her up and down in a theatrical, exaggerated way which I am very good at. Then I pointed my finger at her and said in my best detective inspector voice, 'I see no hay.' I felt her forehead. 'And no fever. I can only conclude, madam, that you are lying.'

Mum didn't laugh. I really was losing my touch. She looked away and stared at the curtains as if they were the most interesting thing she had ever seen.

'You can watch a Harry Hill DVD if you like,' she said.

Mum *NEVER* lets me watch TV until all my homework is done. Something was definitely up.

I usually laugh myself sick watching Harry Hill, but I couldn't concentrate. My mind was racing: Mum had put a lock on the bathroom door, baked buns and, worst of all, cried at my jokes. What did it all mean? And what was going to become of me now? If I couldn't make people laugh any more my whole life plan was ruined: the stand-up circuit, the TV appearances, the big house in the country with the granny flat for Mum. I'd have to rethink it all.

I watched another ten minutes of Harry Hill, hoping for inspiration. When it didn't come, I went off to do my homework. I had to research the Reformation for history but I was too distracted to concentrate so I just sat at the computer and researched Harry Hill instead. I went through his website hoping some of his genius would rub off on me. Mum always says greatness inspires greatness, so I know she would have approved. I felt sure that if I could only get closer to Harry Hill, I'd get my comic touch back.

And that's when I had this brilliant idea.

It took me a while before I found an address where I could contact him. There was one address for his agent and one for fan mail. I decided on his agent. I reckoned he probably gets tonnes of fan mail every week and it would take ages to reach mine, but who in their right mind would want to write to his agent? I took a sheet of paper from the printer and started writing.

You have no idea how hard it is to write to your idol without sounding like a total weirdo. My first attempt started out 'Dear Harry Hill, You don't know me but I know you.' It sounded more like a threat from a psycho-loony stalker than a charming cry for help from a hilarious twelve-year-old boy. In the end, though, I think I did all right.

Dear Harry Hill
I know you must be really busy with all the TV and home videos you have to watch but please, please take a minute to help me. I am a twelve-year-old boy and I plan to be a comedian when I grow up, but recently I've sort of lost my touch. Has anyone ever cried when you told them a joke? If so, how did you overcome the problem? Please write back because I really need help.
    Yours sincerely
    Philip Wright

3

We're No Angels

I promised I'd tell you about Ang's name, didn't I? Well, wait for it: it is Angel. Seriously. And it's pronounced Ang-*hell*. What kind of parents call their child Ang-hell?

'Spanish ones,' he said. 'My dad's name is Angel too. I'm named after him.'

'Blimey,' I said. 'What's your mum called – Saint?'

'Encarnacion,' he said.

I thought that was a weird name too but I didn't say so because, at the time, I hardly knew Ang. He'd just moved into our street and I was trying to be friendly, partly because my mum told me to and partly because it was the summer holidays and there was no-one else around to play football with.

'Ang-hell. That's rough,' I said.

'What's wrong with it?' he said.

'It's a bit sort of – holy,' I said. 'And – um – wing-y.'

I never even saw the punch coming. It landed in my stomach.

Boy! This Ang-hell business really bugged him. And then just to prove it he punched me again. And then I punched him back and – what do you know – we were having an all-out fist fight. Nice way to welcome a new neighbour, don't you think?

We were best friends after that. I got a bloody nose and Ang got a black eye which I was kind of jealous of because a bloody nose isn't that dramatic once the blood's been cleaned up. Whereas a black eye – that has mileage. For days everyone kept asking Ang about his black eye and giving him loads of sympathy and attention. It wasn't fair, because I'd given him the black eye yet he was the one getting all the glory.

After that, we set about solving the Ang-hell problem. We were both starting the same secondary school that September and he said he couldn't take any more where-are-your-wings jokes.

First of all, we tried changing his name to Brian, but every time I called him Brian he just ignored me because he couldn't remember that *he* was actually Brian. That's when we realised it would have to be something closer to his real name.

'What about Angus?' I suggested. I've always liked the name Angus.

'Nah,' Angel said. 'Isn't that the name of a cow?

'That's Aberdeen Angus. Different thing altogether,' I said, thinking this Angus thing could really work.

'Still don't like it,' Angel said. 'Too cowy.'

'You could shorten it,' I said hopefully, 'to Ang.'

He stopped chomping on the chocolate bar he'd been eating (without sharing) and stared at me with a look of cold contempt that was impressive.

'Du-uh!' he said. 'I could shorten my *own* name to Ang.'

'Well, why don't you?' I said.

'Well, I will.'

'Well, do, then.'

'Watch me,' he said and stomped off to find his parents.

His mum didn't like it. She said the whole idea was 'loco'. And asked him why he wanted to shorten his name to Ang.

'Because Ang doesn't *mean* anything,' he said in a slow voice that sounded like he was explaining two plus two to a toddler.

Bad move. His mum started shouting at him in very rapid Spanish. It sounded like a machine gun going off. She could definitely win the world speed-talking championships.

It wasn't long before Ang joined in and was rattling away with his mum. Then his dad came in to the room and he joined in too and the whole thing started to sound worryingly like a great big fight. Obviously, I had no idea what they were saying. The only word I could make out was 'Ang-hell', which they were over-using, in my opinion.

I mean, come on! 'Ang' is not a million miles away from 'Angel'. It's practically the same.

Just then, they all stopped yelling and looked at me. That was when I realised I'd said that last bit out loud.

There was a long silence, then Ang's mum said 'Si,' which even I knew meant yes in Spanish.

Just then Ang's dad started making this rasping sound at the back of his throat like he was going to choke and throwing his arms up in the air as if to say, 'Kill me, I am ready to die.' Which was impressive, if a bit melodramatic.

He was wasting his time. Ang's mum had made her mind up and no amount of choking to death was going to change it. She pinched Ang's cheek and said something decisive-sounding in Spanish (which ended with the word 'Ang') and that was that. Problem solved. Ang wasn't an angel any more.

4
Peeping Tom

It was a week before I saw The Goddess Lucy again. A whole week! It was agony. Ang says I am suffering from unrequited love. He said that Mrs Gray the English teacher read a poem about it last Thursday when I was off getting new specs, and that it means loving someone when they don't love you back. Sounds bang on to me. And, wait for it, Ang said that one of the poems they read was about a girl called Lucy! I reckon it's a sign. Think about it: love, me, poem, Lucy. It all adds up. We were meant to be together.

The problem is, she is only in my art class and we only have art once a week, but I usually see her around the school at break times. I'd been on the lookout for her but I hadn't seen her once. Not even a peek. Maybe she was off sick. Oh my God! I hoped it was nothing serious.

'What if it's something serious?' I said to Ang.

'*You* are something serious,' he said. 'Lucy has turned your brain to mushy peas.'

'What's wrong with mushy peas?' I asked. I like mushy peas. With chips.

'For brain matter?' was all Ang said, as if that somehow

proved his point. Then he went off to look for his PE kit which he'd left behind in one of the classrooms. It was all right for him. Girls liked him. They were always smiling at him and telling him he was cute, even some of the older girls. I couldn't see the attraction myself.

Without Ang I was at a loose end, so I went off to hang around outside the girls' lockers, which is this thing I sometimes do. And before you even think it: No, I am not some kind of Peeping Tom pervert. It's just that I have more chance of running into Lucy outside the girls' lockers than anywhere else. She is always in there gossiping with her annoying friend Holly, sneering, unrequiting me, that sort of thing. Last week I saw her twice.

Unfortunately, she saw me too and called me a Peeping Tom then ran off giggling with her mates. Who was this Tom guy anyway? Probably some innocent young boy trying to steal a glimpse of the one he loved and he ends up getting labelled a pervert. Love is cruel.

There was no sign of Lucy at the girls' lockers and I got fed up being stared at by the other girls with that 'Go away you creep' look, so I decided to give it up and go help Ang find his PE bag. But I didn't get very far because as soon as I turned around I bumped into a six-foot-tall and six-foot-wide wall of a Yeti.

'What are you laughing at, Wright?' he said.

I hate people calling me by my surname. It always makes me want to answer, 'Wrong'.

'Wrong,' I said. 'I wasn't laughing.' Which was true. I wasn't. I was pining.

'Yes, you were. I saw you,' The Yeti said and pushed me back against the lockers.

There was an enormous clang as my head and shoulders hit the metal doors and a gaggle of girls came running out oohing and aahing and wanting to know what was going on. And wouldn't you know it? There was lovely Lucy looking right at me and my feet didn't even touch the ground. This was bad. This was seriously not cool. No-one fancies the boy who is being lifted off the ground by a thug, and whose lips are going blue because the thug's big fat fingers are cutting off their oxygen supply.

Cyanotic! I could just hear the casualty staff call out, *Get the crash trolley.* (I watch a lot of hospital dramas with Mum.)

The Yeti looked over at the girls, smiled through the veil of hair that hung over his hideous face and smashed me against the lockers again. Just for show. My head was really starting to hurt now. But worse, this time my glasses fell off and when I moved to try and get them I nearly choked to death on his grip.

'If I catch you laughing at me one more time, you're dead,' The Yeti said and set me free.

Then he stepped back and on to my specs. My *new* specs. I heard them crack. The girls gasped.

'Oopsy,' The Yeti said and turned to walk away.

I looked at my broken new specs. I looked at Lucy. Then I completely lost it. I forgot that I am a five-foot-nothing, six-stone weakling. I charged after The Yeti and hurled myself at him and I actually managed to knock him down.

Ang says this is because I got him unawares, that I would never ordinarily be able to take him down as I'm not strong enough. Thanks, Ang.

Well, you can imagine the scene: one long-haired Yeti flailing around face down on the floor, all arms and legs waving madly, while a six-stone weakling sat on him. We must have made a real picture because a crowd had gathered and were laughing and clapping and chanting, 'Fight! Fight!'

No! No!

Within seconds The Yeti was up off the floor and had me pinned to the wall again. He was just about to sink his fist into my face when Mr Higgins, the biology teacher, came along.

'Headmaster's office. Now!' he barked and marched us off.

That's when something surreal happened. Instead of yelling at The Yeti and giving him a month of after-school detentions like he should have, the headmaster went all soft. On The Yeti! He didn't even shout at him. He told us he expected more of us. *Us!* I was the victim here. Then, worst of all, he gave The Yeti *one* lunchtime detention. One measly lunchtime detention, while I got an after-school detention, again. How fair is that?

And then something even more surreal and a bit creepy happened. As the headmaster was ushering us out of his office he asked The Yeti how his mother was doing. So that was it. The headmaster had a thing for yeti mamas! Creepalicious. I couldn't wait to tell Ang.

Then I remembered that I had yet another Thursday detention and all the fun went out of it. Mum would go berserk. And I'd broken my new specs. I didn't know how I could face her. And to make matters worse, she had been acting really weird lately, staying off work and bursting in to tears all the time. Every time I asked what was wrong she just said she had hay fever. She obviously thinks I am a total dimwit who can't tell the difference between sneezing and crying. If I told her about The Yeti and the glasses she might crack completely. She was like one of those crazies you see on TV dramas who cry for no good reason, then kill someone. I didn't want that happening.

Especially if the someone was me.

5
Thand Thuckth

You are not going to believe what happened next. The Goddess came up to me in art class! At first I thought I was seeing things because I didn't have my specs. She wasn't dragged or pushed or screaming or anything, so I assumed she had come to make fun of me over the whole Yeti-versus-wimp thing. She just cannot miss an opportunity to sneer. So I wasn't too concerned that I had just put a spoonful of sand in my mouth.

We were making collages so we had a load of art stuff out and Ang had this brilliant idea to cheer me up with an experiment. The idea was to put a spoonful of something in our mouths. I chose sand, he chose glitter. And yes, we did check they were non-toxic before we began. We are not idiots. The object of the experiment was to see how long we could keep each substance in our mouths before we filled up with saliva and had to spit it all out. First to spit loses.

We'd just got started when The Goddess came up to me for her weekly sneer. But you know what? She didn't sneer. She just sort of smiled, reached out her hand to me and said, 'Here. You dropped these.'

Isn't that just about the most romantic thing you've ever heard? I was so light-headed that she was actually talking to me, I didn't even notice what she'd set on the desk. I squinted at her and tried to say something but my mouth was filled with sand, so it was tricky.

'I, uh, Loothy,' I said. 'Ugh. Thand.'

I shut up.

She stared at me.

I started to choke.

That's when I swallowed a tiny sand-saliva cocktail (seriously vomitricious, don't even think about trying it). I started to gag and splutter and *panic*!

What if I choked to death; was love worth that? I imagined my gravestone:

> *Here lie the remains of Philip Wright*
> *who died tragically from eating sand*
> *while concealing its whereabouts*
> *from the woman he loved.*

I held my lips closed tight but still a trickle of saliva managed to escape out the corner of my mouth. And then it happened. I couldn't stop it. (The impulse to breathe and be alive is obviously stronger than the impulse to look cool.) I opened my mouth for air, but that made me gag even more and my tongue shot out and deposited a saliva-coated plop of sand at Lucy's feet.

It looked remarkably like a miniature poo. Lucy stared at it, horrified.

I tried to speak, but you try talking with sand in your mouth – *not* easy. 'Thorry,' was all I managed.

'Be like that,' she said. 'I was only trying to help.'

And she tossed her long golden goddess locks at me and pranced off.

I turned to Ang, who was spitting glitter into a paper towel and laughing himself to death.

'Nice move,' he said. 'Sticking your tongue out at her like that. Thmoooth.'

'Pleathe,' I said. 'I have thand in my mouth and the Goddeth Loothy thinkth I thuck my thongue out at her.'

'You did thick your thongue out at her,' Ang said.

'Thum friend you are,' I said.

And then we both nearly choked laughing.

Then I noticed what Lucy had left on the desk for me. My glasses. She had picked up my glasses after the fight and I hadn't even said thanks. She was back with Holly and her other friends and they were all fussing round her like a family of demented meerkats – looking at her and cooing; shooting suspicious looks over at me, then looking rapidly away again. Lucy's face was all red and thundery looking and Holly, the Chief Meerkat, looked murderous. They are very loyal creatures, meerkats. You've got to admire that in them. Boy! I'd really blown it. A chance in a life time to strike up friendly conversation with The Goddess and I was eating sand like a deranged toddler.

You wouldn't think it was possible, but the day just kept getting worse. Next up was two whole periods of English.

And to make matters even worse, Mrs Gray was

stubbornly refusing to revise the poetry she'd covered last week when I was off. We'd moved on to – wait for it – formal letter writing. I ask you: I am twelve – I couldn't even go on a school trip to the corner shop without my mum's signature. If I need a formal letter written, I'll leave it to her. I don't like to offend so I took down the notes from the board, which was big of me because I could only see out of one side of my specs. I had to keep the other eye closed because the cracked glass made it look like I was seeing everything through a kaleidoscope.

I still hadn't given up hope on the poetry so I looked around the room for signs of unrequited-love poems but I couldn't see any. There were just posters reminding you what a metaphor is and telling you how to spell stuff. That's when I made up my mind – I would ask Mrs Gray for the poetry myself. If Mohammed wouldn't come to the mountain, then the mountain would come to Mohammed. That is a metaphor. See, my education has not been wasted.

When class was over and everybody else had escaped, I hung around to speak to Mrs Gray. She sighed when she saw me.

'Philip Wright interested in poetry!' she said, when I told her what I wanted. 'What's brought this on?'

That's when I started prattling on about how much I love poetry. I could see she wasn't convinced.

'I even write my own poems sometimes,' I lied. 'When nobody's looking,' I added, to make it sound realistic.

'Philip,' she said, smiling, 'aren't you the dark horse!'

A *what* horse? Never mind. Just get the poems.

'Well,' Mrs Gray said eventually, 'it just so happens that I have a few spare copies. I can let you have one of each. This is refreshing.'

Then she went over to her cupboard and handed me a huge wad of papers. She'd obviously mixed the poems up with some sixth former's fifty-million-word essay in the pile so I said, 'Just the poems please.'

'That's it,' she said, beaming at me.

It couldn't be right. I wanted to know about unrequited love but I didn't want to read all that.

'I will be very interested to hear what you think about them,' Mrs Gray said. 'This really is *so* refreshing. Come and see me next Wednesday at the start of lunch period, and bring some of your own poetry. I'd love to read it.'

Her face had gone all pink and she was grinning at me like I was some kind of prize. I wondered if she might be a bit mad.

Ang was waiting for me outside the classroom.

'I write my own poems,' he said in a whining voice that was supposed to sound like me but didn't because I don't whine. 'You are such a prat,' he added.

'A poetry-loving, poet prat,' I said. 'What the heck am I going to do? She wants to read *my* poems. On Wednesday.'

'Better get scribbling,' Ang said.

And he looked so smug I could have punched him.

6

Poetry Thuckth Too

After detention I took the long way home. I had to think. I'd left my specs in school and I hated the idea of lying to Mum about my specs but I hated the idea of telling her the truth even more. Maybe if I just stayed out of her way.

But sure enough, when I opened the front door, there she was waiting for me. Again.

'I need to go to the toilet,' I said. It was all I could come up with at short notice.

'Can't it wait?' she said. 'I've *got* to talk to you.'

'Sorry, Mum, you know how it is,' I said. 'I've *got* to go.'

I ran up the stairs.

Once in the bathroom I was safe. But there's nowhere to sit in a bathroom except the loo. Funny how you don't think of things like that. I put the lid down and sat.

One thing I discovered that day is just how hard toilet seats are. You just can't get comfortable. I sighed and pulled Mrs Gray's poetry out of my schoolbag, but I couldn't concentrate. I felt stupid sitting there in my uniform, like a fully dressed person in a nudist camp. There was only one thing for it. I lifted the toilet lid, pulled down my trousers and under-thingies and sat down properly. Far more natural. I picked up the pages again. Definitely better. And that is how I wound up reading love poetry with my trousers round my ankles.

This unrequited love business is very complicated. And *very* long. Seven whole pages long to be precise. Unfortunately I can read perfectly well without my specs. I couldn't bear it. All I wanted was a kind of *Handy Hints for Unrequited Lovers*, preferably in bullet points. What I'd got was the complete and unabridged ramblings of some dead guys.

There were three poems altogether. The first one was by someone called Keats and was called 'Ode to a Nightingale'. I didn't like the sound of that. I mean, a bird is hardly going to unrequite a human, now, is it? But in fact the poem started out quite promising with the line, 'My heart aches, and a drowsy numbness pains my sense.'

Hmm … not bad. If I just changed the words a bit. I shifted on the toilet seat. 'My bum aches, and a drowsy numbness pains my buttocks.' Mrs Gray was always telling us to find parallels with real life in the work of the great writers. I reckoned she'd be impressed.

I read the rest of the poem, but it might as well have been written in Swahili – I had no idea what the heck it was on about. So I decided to skip out the next seven verses, and as there were only eight verses in the poem that was Keats dealt with. The next poem was by Somebody Gilbert or Gilbert Somebody. I don't know which but I couldn't see any mention of Lucy in his stuff so I ditched that. Great – two down, only one to go.

I turned the page and there she was: Lucy. At last.

It was by someone called Wordsworth. First, I thought, *Ger-roovy name for a poet* and then I thought, *Not groovy*. You should have seen the length of that poem. It went on for pages and pages and pages. I thought the glory of a poem was that it fitted on one page. I was feeling seriously swindled but I read the first line anyway. 'Strange fits of passion have I known ...'

Wow! That bit really spoke to me, because I did once take a coughing fit in the canteen when Lucy sat down opposite me and I was so lovestruck that my mango and pomegranate smoothie went down the wrong way and nearly killed me.

The rest of the poem did not speak to me – or, if it did, I had no idea what it was saying. As far as I could make out some guy rides past his girlfriend's house one moonlit night and thinks, *OMG! What if she's, like, dead?* I was beginning to think maybe Wordsworth was simple. I mean who goes around imagining their girlfriend is dead for no good reason? But then I read these lines:

I to her cottage bent my way
Beneath an evening moon.

Now, I don't know about you, but I call that stalking. If I crept round to Lucy's house in the moonlight and hung around outside her window, she'd probably have me arrested. And another thing. Wordsworth would need to learn how to write a sentence. If in language back to front wrote I, the teacher kill me would. And it kept getting worse because the more I read, the less I understood, and my buttocks felt like they were glued to the toilet seat and were starting to get a bit numb, and Mrs Gray was going to ask me all about it (the poetry not my butt) and … *Help!*

Just then my mobile went. It was Ang. What do you know? You just have to call out for help and help comes!

'You're psychic,' I said.

'Am I?' he said, sounding surprised. 'You'd think I'd know that much then.'

He was eating crisps. I could tell by the deafening crunch. Food is the love of Ang's life. I didn't say too much about it before because he is self-conscious about his weight and I didn't like to draw attention to it. I thought I could hear Mum outside the door again so I lowered my voice.

'I need your help,' I whispered to Ang.

'Why are you whispering?' he asked.

'Because I'm on the toilet.'

'Yeuch!' he groaned. 'You've put me off my crisps.'

'Ang,' I pleaded, 'you've got to help me.'

'You want me to come and rescue you from the toilet?'

'Poetry sucks,' I said, trying to ignore his chomping.

'What do you want me to do about it?' Ang mumbled through his crisps.

'Explain it,' I said.

'How should I know?' Ang said. 'I'm no poet.'

'You were there that day in class.'

'So? I was there when I was born but I don't remember any of that.'

You cannot argue with logic like that so I didn't argue.

'You said this Lucy poem was good,' I accused him.

'No I never. I said it was about someone called Lucy.'

'Ang, you told me it was about unrequited love.'

'No I didn't. I said we did a poem about unrequited love and that we did a poem about someone called Lucy. I don't know which is which. We did another poem as well but I can't remember what it was about.'

'Sore buttocks,' I said.

'Really? You'd think I'd remember that.'

I was starting to think maybe Ang knew as little about the poems as I did.

'Listen,' I said. 'Finish your crisps and focus. What is the Lucy poem about?'

'Dunno.'

'Try! This is important.'

'OK.' Ang swallowed loudly. 'I *think* Mrs Gray said Wordsworth wrote this poem about nature or love or something. And that he was obsessed with Lucy but that she might be a figment of his imagination or an idea or something.'

An idea! 'You mean Lucy wasn't even real?' That's when I lost all respect for Wordsworth. I mean, who invents girlfriends that might possibly be *ideas* for themselves? I could hear Ang munching away on his crisps again without a care in the world and I wanted to throttle him. Maybe he'd got it wrong. 'God, Ang! *concentrate*,' I squawked. 'Help meeee!'

I must have shouted that last bit because Mum came thundering up the stairs and started banging on the door.

I was so startled I nearly wet myself. Which wasn't really a problem because I was sitting on the toilet, but still, you like to be in full control of your bladder, don't you?

'Philip. Are you all right?' she said through the door. Her voice was all panicky.

Seriously, what did she think could happen to me sitting on the toilet?

'Let me in,' she squawked.

Let me remind you: I am twelve years old, nearly thirteen. I do not need help with my toilet activities.

'Go away!' I hissed at her.

'Be like that,' Ang said all huffy.

'Not you,' I explained. 'Her.'

'Her?' Ang squawked. 'Have you got a girl in there with you?'

'Shut up you pervert!' It was my turn to squawk.

'Don't you speak to me like that,' Mum cried. 'You come out here right now.'

'I'm sorry,' I said. 'I didn't mean you.'

But she wouldn't listen. She started banging on the door again.

'Go away!' I yelled.

'That's it,' Ang said. 'I've had enough.' But he didn't hang up.

Just then Mum began to cry. Real big choky sobs. 'I didn't bring you up to talk to me like that,' she wailed. 'I'm under a lot of stress at the minute,' she sobbed. 'I need your help and ...' (sob) ' ... love.' And then she blew her nose. It sounded like an elephant being slaughtered.

'I'm sorry,' I said. 'You know I love you.'

'You what!' Ang screeched down the phone.

'Not you, you creep,' I said.

'Who are you calling a creep?' Mum said and started bawling all over again.

I was thinking the only way out of the situation would be to put my head down the toilet and pull the flush, when the doorbell rang.

'Who's that?' Mum said, sounding a bit panicked.

'How the heck should I know? In case you hadn't noticed *I am on the toilet!*'

The doorbell went again and the person outside lifted the letter flap.

'Yoo hoo! Kathy, let me in,' the person cooed. 'I come bearing gifts.'

It was Susie, Mum's best friend. Hallelujah. Mum blew her nose again and went down to let her in.

I lifted my phone and said to Ang, 'Now, about Wordsworth …'

But he was gone.

7
Hair Frighteners

Once I knew it was Susie down there I knew it would be safe to come out. She always puts Mum in a good mood. I bolted down the stairs, then walked calmly into the living room, trying not to look like someone who indulged in bare-bum poetry recitals. Mum and Susie stopped talking when they saw me.

'How's my favourite comedian?' Susie said.

'What do you call a man with a seagull on his head?' I asked her.

'Cliff,' she said. 'You'll have to do better than that.'

'OK,' I said, rising to the challenge. 'What do you call a man with bananas in both ears?'

'Haven't you got homework to do?' Mum said, interrupting me. Mum is very keen on homework.

'Wait,' Susie said, 'until your mum opens her presents.'

'Presents?' I said dumbly, like I'd never heard the word before.

'Presents?' Mum said like she was trying to outdo me in the stupid stakes.

'Pres-ents,' Susie said like she was translating at a National Institute for Idiots Convention. 'You know, gift wrapped in paper, given on special occasions.' And she handed over a bag to Mum. 'Belated happy birthday to you,' she sang. 'Happy birthday, dear Kathy, happy birthday to you.'

'That was a month ago,' Mum said.

'So? I was away. Open!'

Mum removed a bottle-shaped present from the bag which, when unwrapped, turned out to be a bottle. Full of her favourite wine. Mum smiled. Good old Susie. Mum loves presents. She lifted a longish, rectangular box from the bag. It looked like it might contain a new controller for my games console. I grinned. Mum grinned – all traces of the dreaded piggy eyes gone.

Susie had obviously put quite an effort into the wrapping because there was a lot of tape on it and Mum had to bite at it with her teeth. So there was Mum grinning and gnawing away at her present as happy as a beaver with a log and for the first time in a week I felt like things were normal again. Not that my mother going around gnawing things is the norm; I just mean she had stopped being serious for half a second and whatever it was that was bothering her vanished.

'Careful,' Susie said. 'I don't want to have to pay for replacement dentures!'

Mum laughed and eventually managed to tear off the paper. 'Hair straighteners!' she announced.

Not the most exciting present in the world, I think you'll agree. I have to admit I was a teensy bit disappointed but I kept on grinning, just for show. Anyway, Mum would be pleased. She'd been going on about getting a set of straighteners for ages.

But you know what she did? She burst into tears and ran out of the room and up the stairs and locked herself in the bathroom.

Susie and I looked at each other. We could hear Mum sobbing.

'Why don't you go round to Ang's?' Susie suggested.

And even though my mum was locked in a bathroom bawling like a baby, I thought, *Cool*. I never get to go round to Ang's on a week night because of homework.

I was out the door like a shot.

8

Ha-Lucy-nations

On the way round to Ang's I rang him from my mobile to let him know I was coming.

'On a week night?' he asked. 'Has your mother taken leave of her senses?'

How did he know?

'It's a treat for her birthday,' I lied. I didn't want him to know that my mother had, in fact, lost her mind and was locked in the loo because she had developed a sudden and worrying fear of hair-styling equipment. 'Can I come round or can't I?'

'OK,' Ang said. 'But no poetry and no telling me you love me. Deal?'

'Deal,' I said.

As I was stuffing my mobile back into my pocket I noticed a girl in a blue hoodie standing at the corner of the street who looked remarkably like Lucy. I can honestly say that was the first time I really missed my specs. I could cope with not being able to see the board at school, no sweat, but now I couldn't even bring the love of my life into focus. The weird thing is, Lucy doesn't live anywhere near me and she is a complete swot so there was no chance she'd be out on a week night. There was only one possible explanation: I was hallucinating. Ha-Lucy-nating to be precise. See what love does to you? It makes you mentally deranged.

Still, even a hallucination of Lucy was better than nothing and I couldn't help thinking, *If only she were mine*. I sat on the wall outside Ang's house to let the thought sink in and before I knew it, I'd composed a poem about her. I think you'll agree that writing a poem based on a hallucination of a girl who didn't even love me in the first place shows great skill and imagination. But even though I'd actually succeeded in composing a poem I still felt a bit sick in my stomach. Because, the truth is – I meant that poem. And I knew I'd have to write it down quickly or I'd forget it, so I got up and rang Ang's doorbell.

His mum greeted me by patting me on the head and pinching my cheek like I was a cross between a Labrador and a toddler. I must really be adorable to have this effect on Ang's mum. She smiled at me and said something in Spanish.

'What did she say?' I asked Ang when I got to his room, where he was sitting at his computer.

'*Donde hay amor, hay dolor*,' he said without turning round.

'In English, *please*,' I said.

'It's a Spanish proverb,' Ang said. 'It means where there is love, there is pain.'

'You told her!' I squawked.

'Told her what? There is nothing to tell.'

'About Lucy.'

'Are you nuts?' Ang said. 'I don't have to tell her anything. You've got it written all over your face. You're like a great big miserable bloodhound.'

'Bloodhound, really?' I said. 'I was thinking more – cuddly Labrador.'

'Poodle,' Ang said.

'Get off. I am not a poodle.'

And then we started making dog noises, howling and barking and performing dog tricks until I remembered I wasn't a dog, I was a poet and I needed to write my poem down before I forgot.

'Sit,' I said.

Ang sat. Maybe I'll become a dog trainer when I grow up.

'Type this up,' I said, but he ignored me this time.

'Quick, before I forget.'

'I'm not your slave,' Ang said and stared at his computer. He can be seriously stubborn when he wants.

'Do you have paper in the printer?'

'Hmm?' he said, staring at some girl's Facebook page.

'*A-ang*!' I pleaded, 'this is a matter of life and death.'

He stopped staring at the computer and swivelled round to look at me. (He was on a swivel chair just in case you're visualising a strange Spanish child with a 360°-swivel-function neck joint.)

'Whose life or death?' he asked.

'Mine,' I said, and before he had time to turn back to his computer I added, 'I did it. I wrote a love poem for Mrs Gray.'

'For Mrs Gray! Are you in love with *her* now?'

'No, you freak. It's *about* Lucy, but it's *for* Mrs Gray.'

'You are going to give your Lucy love poem to Mrs Gray?' Ang said looking worried. 'Don't you think that'll send her the wrong kind of message?'

'Oh, hilarious,' I said. 'She thinks I'm a poet, remember? Come on, it'll only take a minute.'

Ang groaned but turned round to the keyboard.

'I said no poetry, but OK, go!' he said.

I cleared my throat and announced, 'If she were mine.'

I paused for dramatic effect.

Ang turned round. 'Is that it?'

'That,' I said scornfully, 'is the title.'

Then I recited the whole poem from start to finish and Ang rattled away on the keyboard, and he didn't even snort or scoff once – told you it was good. When he was finished typing, he printed off a copy and we both stared at the finished product:

If she were mine
My eyes would shine.
I'd sing out loud
And be so proud.
If she were mine
It'd be so fine.
I'd dance around
And give beggars a pound.
If she were mine I wouldn't stalk
I'd go right up and talk.
If she were mine.

'That is *so* lame,' Ang said.

'*That* is my soul you're talking about,' I said.

'Anyway,' Ang said, 'don't poems have to be all weird, and not be about what they are really about? And don't you have to use weird language like *thee* and *thou*?'

'I'm writing a poem,' I said, 'not time-travelling.'

Ang handed me the poem. 'What's the big rush, anyway?' he said. 'I thought you had until next Wednesday.'

'Trust me, you don't want to know,' I said.

'Go on,' Ang said. 'You know you want to tell me.'

How did he know that? I was beginning to think that maybe Ang really was psychic.

'I won't have time next week,' I confessed. 'I think my mother is having a mental breakdown, so I will be busy next week visiting her in a top-security mental hospital.'

'Wow!' Ang said. 'What are the signs?'

'She bakes cakes and cries a lot.'

'No way! So does mine.' He looked delighted.

I could tell he wasn't taking this seriously.

'Do you think my mum might be mad too?' he asked.

I gave this some thought then concluded, 'Your mum may be mad, but if she is, she is mad all the time because she hasn't changed, which means she is normal-mad because that is normal for her.'

'Normal-mad?'

'Yes,' I said decisively, 'but *my* mum normally buys cakes from shops and normally laughs like a hyena all of the time. So this baking and crying business is really abnormal and means that she is worryingly mad.'

'I see,' said Ang. And I thought maybe he did see because he looked very serious. Then he said, 'They'll have to lock her up, away from any baking utensils, in case she tries to harm herself with a spatula.'

'Oh. My. God,' I said. 'A spatula attack. That alone is probably a criminal offence.'

'High risk,' Ang added. 'Category A.'

'High-security unit for sure,' I said. 'With guard dogs and barbed wire fences in case she tries to dig her way out with a wooden spoon and bake some fairy cakes.'

'Or muffins,' Ang suggested.

'Brownies.'

'Flapjacks,' Ang said with tears in his eyes.

And we both fell about laughing and shouting out the names of all the cakes we could think of.

After that I felt a whole lot better.

But on my way back home I saw my haLucynation again, and this time it was talking to another person in a hoodie. And the other hoodied person was a boy. Oh my God! My hallucination was cheating on me.

I was immediately plunged into despair. It's true what they say: love really is a rollercoaster of emotion. One minute you're all smiles, writing poetry and the next you're miserable and considering beating up the hallucination that is talking to your imaginary girlfriend. It would wear you out.

This is not how I imagined love would be. Once when I was watching a soppy film with Mum about a boy who finds comfort in his first love after his dog dies (the dog bit was good), Mum said to me, 'Just you wait until you fall in love. It will be so wonderful.' Shows you how much she knows. Maybe back in the old days when Mum was in love things were different. Back then girls probably wore pigtails, and boys carried their bags home from school. Well, things are different in the modern world. Just supposing Lucy would even let me near her bag; do you know how much the average schoolbag weighs in the first part of the twenty-first century? If I were to attempt to carry both our bags home from school I'd end up with severe curvature of the spine, and then I'd be a five-foot-nothing, six-stone specky guy with a stoop.

Take it from me: modern love is hell.

9

Insomnia

Susie met me at the front door.

'Aww,' she said, 'what's wrong, do you want a hug?'

Being in love was bad but it wasn't that bad.

'*No way!*' I said, pushing past her.

'Ouch!' Susie said. She looked a bit hurt. That's when I noticed her eyes were really red. So she had developed pig-eye syndrome too. It must be catching.

'Come on,' she said, 'cheer up and have some chips. I can't cope with two Wrights being wrong.'

Get it? Two Wrights – me and Mum. That is an old joke of Susie's that I usually pretend to find funny, but tonight I hadn't the heart.

'What's wrong with the other Wright?' I said, stuffing my mouth with chips.

'She's in bed,' Susie said. 'She's really not feeling very well so she's having a sleep.' Then she added, 'And don't talk with your mouth full. It is beyond revolting.'

Adults are unbelievable. My Mum was possibly mentally unstable, and all Susie could think about was my table manners.

'Can I go up and see her?' I asked. 'After I've finished my chips.'

'She's worn out, Philip. I think we should let her sleep.'

'What's wrong with her?' I asked again. 'She's been acting really weird.'

Susie choked on one of her chips, then said, 'Oh, I forgot. Your mum said you could watch one of your Harry Hill recordings and eat your dinner off your knees tonight.'

'Then what are we waiting for?' I said.

Susie stayed until I'd finished my homework and had my shower and was supposedly ready for bed. I tried telling her I didn't usually go to bed until midnight but she wouldn't listen. She made me go to bed at nine-thirty and checked that I had her phone number in my mobile. She told me to keep it on and phone her if we needed anything.

'Mum doesn't let me keep my phone on at night,' I told her.

'And you always do what Mum says, do you?'

'She says I'll get brain damage or head cancer or something,' I said.

'Oh!' Susie said. 'Well, in that case just switch it on if you need me.'

She looked a bit flustered, but I didn't really think she should take that stuff too seriously. I think Mum just made it up to stop me having my phone at night.

After Susie let herself out I went in to Mum's room to see how she was, but she was fast asleep with the light off so I went back to my own room and got into bed. Nine-thirty: I had a long night ahead of me.

By midnight I must have counted over two million sheep, and I'd decided that I definitely do not want to be a sheep farmer when I grow up. It looks glamorous on those Australian documentaries, but when you've spent hours in bed with millions of sheep, the glamour kinda wears thin.

At two AM I crept out of bed and in to Mum's room; she was still asleep. I could tell because apart from the closed eyes and the lifeless body, she was snoring a bit. There was a box of pills on her bedside cabinet. They were new. I tried to see what was on the label but it was too dark. Probably vitamins. Mum's always going on about vitamins.

I stood in her doorway and made another new discovery: your house is a very lonely place when you are the only one awake. I didn't like this discovery. It led to a very unsettling train of thought: to The Yeti and my broken specs and detention and Mrs Gray's poetry and Lucy.

And my feet were cold.

If Mum had been awake she'd have cheered me up. I stood there in the dark remembering how, when I was small and couldn't sleep, she used to get my teddy Sir Fluffington and cuddle me back into bed. Those days were long over, and now Mum was going mad. I shivered. Poor Mum. That's when I decided to give in to the temptation to write to Harry Hill again. I didn't want to pester him or look like a stalker who doesn't even wait for a reply in between letters, but I was desperate.

Dear Harry Hill

You haven't had time to reply to my first letter yet, but I just thought I would update you on what's been happening. My mum only has to look at me now and she bursts into tears. She doesn't even wait to find out if my joke will be any good. I'm getting desperate. Please advise.

Yours sincerely

Philip Wright

PS I know it's not your area of expertise, but if you have any hints on dealing with unrequited love or advice on writing poetry, I'd really appreciate it.

10

Clean Crazy

I heard the sound of hoovering. I checked my watch and saw that it was only six-thirty AM so I reckoned I had to be dreaming. My mother has many faults but cleaning the house at the crack of dawn is not one of them.

'Dammit!' I heard Mum say to the hoover. 'Work properly, can't you?'

So I wasn't dreaming.

'It can't understand you,' I called out. 'It's an inanimate object.'

I dragged myself downstairs. 'What are you doing?' I yawned.

'Cleaning,' she said.

'Du-uh!' I said. 'But why now, at six o'clock in the morning?'

'Don't exaggerate, Philip,' she said. 'It's already gone six-thirty.' She sounded really snappy.

I decided to put the kettle on. Maybe if I made her a cup of tea she'd sit down and tell me what was going on. Perhaps we were going on holiday. Mum always cleans the house from top to bottom before we go on holiday. She likes to leave it nice and clean for the burglars. I wondered where we were going. Somewhere warm, I bet. Mum loves the sun.

After I'd put the kettle on I planned on lining up all the cereal packets on the table and reading the backs of them. But then I remembered I had no specs. You see the ripple effect of The Yeti's actions? Chaos theory.

I said I liked to line up *all* the cereal packets, but these days it is usually just two: muesli and porridge oats (which is really just muesli with the muesli taken out). Mum has become a bit of a health nut when it comes to food and stuff. She's become obsessed with eating five a day and not eating foods that contain sugar and salt and trans fats, whatever they are. Mum is also obsessed with switching off mobiles and the wifi and making me walk places when I could just as easily take a bus. Now she had developed a new obsession: early-morning cleaning. I made the tea, then sat down to my cereal and watched her.

'Have some tea,' I said.

'No time,' she said. 'This place is filthy.'

'It'll still be filthy when you've had your tea,' I said cheerfully.

'Oh ha ha! Mr Bloody Comedian,' Mum said in this really ugly voice. 'If you've finished your breakfast get upstairs and tidy your room.'

I didn't finish my cereal after that. Mum never swears at me. She says swearing is for ruffians with impoverished vocabularies. Mum likes extensive vocabularies – that's why mine is so well developed. She keeps on shoving words down my throat, like omega-three fish oils. She says it's good for me. Well, I could think of a few choice words to say to her that morning. I went upstairs silently mouthing all the swear words I knew and then I just wanted to cry. That is the first time I had actually wanted to swear at Mum.

I went in to her room. I don't know why. I think I was hoping to see some trace of Nice Mum, not the crazy lady who was downstairs cleaning and swearing. And you know what? Her own room was a mess: there were scrunched-up tissues everywhere – on the floor, in the bin, on the floor beside the bin. Her bedside cabinet was the worst – there was a big pile of soggy tissues and four undrunk cups of tea. I sat down on her bed for a minute. It was still warm. I looked at the clock. It wasn't even seven yet. Loads of time.

If I was going to commune with the spirit of Nice Mum what better place to do it than in her great big cosy bed? I pulled back the covers and there was Sir Fluffington staring up at me with his one eye. He lost the other eye in a deadly battle with next door's psychotic Chihuahua when I was five. Have you ever heard the expression 'Time heals all wounds'? Well, take it from me; it doesn't. It has been seven years since the Battle of Wounded Eyeball, and I still regard that dog and his owner (for ever after known as Mrs Chihuahua) as the enemy.

I looked down at Sir Fluffington. Mum must have been feeling nostalgic for the old days too, because she doesn't normally take a teddy bear to bed. I yawned and realised I'd had less than four hours sleep. And you know what they say, children need a lot of sleep for development. Well, I didn't want to be underdeveloped so I got into bed, took one great big sniff of Sir Fluff's head (it smelled of memories) and snuggled down. Within minutes I was fast asleep.

I woke to the sound of Mum yelling at me. 'What are you doing in my bed?' she shrieked.

It was like being in a cheap TV remake of the Goldilocks story and I had the starring role, only I wasn't a girl and I didn't have golden locks. Mum was so cross and stupefied that I actually thought she was going to explode. Her face was purple and a vein was pulsing on the side of her forehead, like a worm had found its way in there and was trying desperately to find its way out again. Seriously unattractive. If the Three Bears looked anything like that it's no wonder Goldilocks threw herself from a top-floor window. I leapt out of bed and ran from the room.

Mum was still cleaning when I left for school. She stopped dusting for half a second and came to the front door. 'Where are your glasses?' she said.

'They're broken,' I said. So much for the clever web of lies I'd planned.

'They're *what*?' The worm in her forehead started pulsing again.

'They're bloody well broken,' I said, and felt my face boil.

'Don't you swear at me,' she snapped.

'Yeah, well. Don't *you* swear at *me*.'

I left her there on the doorstep in a nightie, with a duster in her hand. Her eyes were all bulgy like she'd had no sleep even though she'd been on a mega sleepathon, and her hair was uncombed so she looked like one of those Gorgon monsters with snakes growing out of its head. I really hope no-one saw her.

I usually call for Ang on the way to school but I didn't that day. I was too depressed. I trudged off, walking d-e-a-d s-l-o-w. My feet felt like they were made of lead. Can your emotions affect your body mass? Because I am sure I weighed twice what I had the night before. I felt so heavy. Then I remembered Harry Hill – he might not have written back yet but I could easily recall every one of his jokes about wacko, crazy mums. So I did. And that cheered me right up.

It's good to know you are not alone.

11

Fatso and Pratso

You are never going to believe what happened next, but I am going to tell you anyway.

When I got into school I dragged Ang down to the girls' lockers because I desperately needed cheered up and I thought a glimpse of The Goddess might just do it. I even put my broken specs on so I could see her properly. And you know what? I did.

Talking to The Yeti!

He was towering over her and looked even uglier than ever. I nearly lost my mind.

I grabbed Ang's arm. 'Look! The Yeti is threatening Lucy. What'll we do?'

'Uh, thank God it's not *you*,' Ang said and took out a bar of chocolate.

But I had to do something.

I would go over there and punch that big creep. I would knock him out. I would save Lucy and then maybe she would be really grateful and maybe fall in love with me. Maybe.

'I'm going in,' I said.

'No way!' Ang said, choking on his chocolate.

'*Way!*'

'Cool!' Ang said. 'Can I watch?'

I took a deep breath, pushed my glasses up my nose and marched up to The Yeti. Then, just as I raised my hand to tap him on the shoulder, Lucy glared at me in horror. Poor Lucy. I'd be horrified too if a creep like that was breathing down my neck.

The Yeti turned and snorted. 'Well, if it isn't Fatso and Pratso.'

The Goddess giggled nervously.

It was obvious who was Pratso and who was Fatso because I am ultra thin in an attractive, stick-insect kind of way, and Ang is a tiny bit plump in a non-stick-insect kind of way. This was bad. Really bad. Ang hates it when people comment on his size. I did tell you he was sensitive about it. The thing is, he isn't fat really, just a bit round and soft, like a Teletubby but without the television screen for a stomach. And, he wasn't about to let a big (and genuinely fat) oaf like The Yeti call him Fatso.

He was going to do something stupid. I could feel it.

I was right. Just as The Yeti was making himself a nice big fist-shaped fist, Ang stepped out from behind me and said, 'I have three words for you, Yeti-man: pot, kettle and black.'

'Huh?' The Yeti said, looking to me for explanation.

I looked at Ang. He was about to get his face pulped by fourteen stone of Yeti and all he was worried about was kitchenware. I scratched my head and that's when I remembered I was wearing my broken glasses. In front of Lucy! We had to get away.

'*What?*' I mouthed desperately to Ang.

'You know,' he said, 'the pot calling the kettle black. People in glass houses not throwing stones and stuff.'

Glass houses? Now he'd moved on to gardening. Isn't fear a strange and powerful thing, the way it can make you lose your mind like that?

The Yeti and I stared at him like he was speaking Japanese.

'Huh?' The Yeti said again.

My granda Joe used to talk crazy stuff like this before he died, but he was suffering from dementia, so he had an excuse. He'd been a boxing coach and Mum said that he'd got damaged from too many blows to the head.

Hey! That was it! Ang was suffering from brain damage.

'Wow!' I said to The Yeti. 'You are good. *A-mazing*. You haven't even laid a finger on him and already he's suffering from concussion.'

And – holy saucepan lids! – The Yeti laughed. He opened his great big slimy Yeti mouth and roared. Then he forgot all about pummelling us to death and walked off chortling to himself.

And then – wait for it – The Goddess turned to Ang and me. I reckoned she was warming up for a sneer because Holly and The Meerkats were watching from the entrance to the girls' lockers. But you know what? I didn't care. I had defused a serious Yeti situation without bloodshed and I was so impressed with myself that I was considering a career in conflict resolution. I think there really is such a job.

Anyway, The Goddess stood before us, swished back her hair in that excruciatingly exquisite way she has and said, 'We don't think you're fat, Ang – just sort of cuddly.' She looked at me. 'And I don't think you're a prat,' she said. 'At least, hardly ever.'

Then she swished her hair again and walked off.

Ang stared at me. He was smiling. A lot.

'I'm not fat,' he said. 'I'm *cud-lee*.'

'And I am not a prat,' I said.

I walked around for the rest of the day feeling two stone lighter than I had that morning. Somebody really should do some research into the relationship between mood and body mass. I was so light and happy that I actually felt like skipping, but I didn't because I am not a complete lunatic. Still, you have to admit that things were looking up. I couldn't wait to tell Harry Hill.

Dear Harry Hill

I hope you are well and not sick or seriously injured. I only say this because I've written twice now and you still haven't written back. I thought I'd let you know that I had a breakthrough today. I made a bully laugh. After that, he left me alone.

Have you noticed how people can't look really scary when they are laughing? Weird.

Otherwise, my problems haven't gone away – Mum is still acting weird and I still need help with the poetry. So I would be really grateful if you could hurry up and write back as quickly as possible.

Yours sincerely
Philip Wright

12
Saint Philip

You'd think after a day like that nothing could ruin my good mood. Well, you'd be wrong.

When I got home from school I found the front door open and Susie's car in the driveway. Inside the house there were boxes all over the place. Mum was bent over one of them rummaging through it. She was wearing her nightie tucked into a pair of old jeans and her hair was in the same crazy Gorgon mess as it had been that morning. *Plus* she had no make-up on.

Let me tell you about my mum: she is vain. I mean, if letting your only beloved son slave away making breakfast while you put your make-up on and blow-dry your hair isn't vain, then I don't know what is. Mum never leaves the house without full make-up and hair. Once, when we'd slept in and were late, she nearly crashed the car when she slammed on the brakes and yelled, 'Oh my God! I've forgotten my face!'

She very nearly caused a pile-up. But she didn't, so it was unfair of the driver behind us to get out of his car and shout at Mum and tell her she was a stupid idiot woman. She wasn't stupid; she was vain.

Anyway, the point is, for Mum to be up and about without her 'face' on and sporting crazy hair and PJs in the middle of the afternoon was a sure sign that things were seriously very *very* bad.

Susie came out of the kitchen carrying a box.

'We're off to the dump,' Mum said. 'Wanna come?'

'You're in your nightie,' I said. 'People do not go out in their pyjamas unless they're sleepwalking or they've just escaped from a lunatic asylum.'

Susie opened her mouth to speak but Mum silenced her with one of her looks.

She turned back to me. 'Suit yourself,' she said. And they left.

Without me.

I didn't know what to do then, so I wandered aimlessly round the house which was so clean I hardly recognised it. I felt rotten – I love going to the dump and they'd gone without me – but most of all, being mean to Mum was no fun, even though I was in the right. I resolved to make it up with Mum as soon as she got back. And then I saw my room.

It was spotless.

Yes, I will admit that the room needed tidied. Yes, it had got really bad. Yes, there may have been a slice or two of pizza mouldering under a heap of stinky socks – but that did not give Mum the right to go marauding through my things. I don't suppose marauders tidy up after themselves, but you know what I mean. The whole room was in order: books were on shelves, clothes were in drawers and my shoes were all neatly lined up in pairs. If a TV detective came in to this room he would say a serial killer lived there. TV serial killers are always neat freaks. That's how you can spot them. They're always trying to keep things in order; then they lose control and kill loads of untidy people. I know this because I saw it on *CSI* once.

I looked around my serial killer's room and that's when I saw it: a sheet of paper neatly folded up on my pillow. I recognised the page immediately and felt my stomach lurch.

Mum had read my poem. My *love* poem. To a *girl*.

I was so cross I considered running away, just to teach Mum a lesson. But I knew that was stupid. I had nowhere to go and no money and no running-away stuff. I didn't even own a sleeping bag. Besides, I like my comforts, you know, like food and a bed.

That got me thinking about all those poor people you see sleeping in shop doorways and begging on the street. Their mums must have been really mean to them to make them choose that life. I resolved there and then that the next time I passed one of those people, I would give them some of Mum's money, and maybe even some of her unwanted junk. And that's when I had this amazing idea.

I filled two rucksacks with Mum's cast-offs from the boxes in the hall. There were clothes and books and kitchen things and a whole load of other stuff. There were even some things belonging to Dad, so you can tell how often Mum did a clear out. I found an old jacket of his, some shirts, two ties and some underpants. I didn't think anyone would want someone else's icky underpants so I left those behind. But I took the ties because I thought they could come in handy for tying up wounds to stop bleeding. You know the way they do in films.

I grabbed my keys and wrote Mum a note. *Gone out* was all it said, which was nicely pointless because it would be obvious that I'd gone out since I wouldn't be in. I left my mobile beside the note so Mum would know she couldn't contact me. I thought that was a clever and hurtful thing to do because I knew she would be worried. Well, tough. I was fed up being the one doing all the worrying around here. It was her turn.

It was just after four when I got into town and I was a bit worried that it was too early to find the homeless people, but then I saw an old man sitting in the doorway of a closed-down newsagent's.

'Hi,' I said cheerfully.

He didn't answer.

It hadn't occurred to me that conversation would be a problem.

I couldn't think of anything to say to him so I told him a joke. A golden oldie. You can never go wrong with a classic. 'What do you get if you cross a chicken with a cement mixer?'

'Wha'?' the man said.

'A brick layer,' I said and the old man smiled.

I did a little dance around him, then spread my arms out and said, 'Ta daa! I used to be a tap dancer but I kept falling in the sink.'

The man's smile widened. He couldn't help himself. I *am* very funny.

'Um,' I said, 'would you like a scarf or a hat or maybe a nice book to read?'

The man looked at me like I was barmy, but when I started to take stuff out of the bags he realised I was serious. In the end he took a scarf, both ties (he must really live in fear of bleeding to death), Dad's old jacket, and a pair of ski socks. He looked especially pleased with the jacket. I felt good then. Really good. Like being a saint or something. I think maybe I'll become a monk or a missionary if the comedy doesn't work out.

'What are you doing?' a girl's voice said.

I turned around and couldn't believe my eyes. It was The Goddess. I am SO glad I'd decided not to wear my broken specs.

'What are you doing?' she asked again.

'Nothing,' I managed to say.

'You're not doing nothing; you gave that old man clothes. I saw you.'

'Um, I …'

'Can I help?' she said.

'I, um …'

'I'll take that as a yes,' she said, lifting one of my rucksacks and marched off.

The next person we met was a woman selling paper flowers down near the post office. She didn't speak much English so a joke was out of the question, but eventually, with lots of miming and gesturing, she realised what we were on about.

She took one of Dad's shirts, a jumper, a woolly hat and a baby blanket. The woman gave Lucy one of her paper flowers, which I half expected her to sneer at, because her dad is rich and she can have real flowers any day of the week if she wants them. But she actually looked really pleased with it. I liked Lucy for liking the flower. It made her less goddessy.

After that we met a man with a dog. He looked quite young, about nineteen maybe (the man not the dog). I felt a bit creeped out by him. He had a mean look on his face and he made a low noise in his throat which made the dog growl. Neither Lucy nor I moved.

'Never seen a dog before?' he said.

'Of course,' I said, trying not to sound scared, then added in a *very* squeaky voice, 'My dog is really badly behaved; he chases everyone on a bike.'

'Yeah?' the man said through his mean looking teeth.

'So I took his bike away,' I said and smiled weakly.

The man bent down to his dog.

'Did you hear that, Pip? The boy's a comedian.' When he lifted his head again, he was smiling.

We showed the man what we had left. He took a hand-knitted blanket for Pip to lie on and that book about staying calm from Mum's inner-peace phase.

When we'd left him Lucy said, 'My mum would kill me if she knew what I was doing.'

'Where does she think you are now?'

'Swimming,' she said, pointing to the swim bag slung over her shoulder.

'Why aren't you?' I asked.

'Du-uh! Because I'm here with you.'

I went a bit pink in the face and dived into the rucksack. 'Let's see what's left.'

'I wish I had something to give people,' Lucy said. 'When I go home I'm going to gather up all the things my family never use and give them to people. Redistribution of wealth – my dad'll kill me.' And she burst out laughing, as though getting killed by her dad was the most fun a person could have.

Being with Lucy was amazing. I could not believe my luck, *and* she had the bright idea to go down by the river, where we met a big group of homeless people. They were all crouched together having a laugh about something. I hoped it wasn't me because I hadn't said anything funny yet.

We left them everything – socks, shirts, mittens, a pack of cards and a salad spinner. One of the men put the salad spinner on his head.

'Why did the tomato blush?' I said.

'Because it saw the salad dressing,' the man with the salad spinner hat said.

And we all laughed. All except one girl who was sitting apart from the group.

'She didn't get anything,' Lucy said.

'There's nothing left,' I said, holding up the empty rucksacks.

Lucy screwed up her face. Then she took her swimming bag from her shoulder. She pulled out a very fluffy, very pink towel and a tub of some kind of cream that looked like it came from a really posh shop. She handed the things to the girl.

'Lush,' the girl said opening the tub and taking a sniff.

Lucy turned to me and smiled. The most beautiful smile in the world.

13

Blind Man's Bluff

I take it all back. Love *is* wonderful. I was delirious. And if my body-mass/mood theory was anything to go by, I must have weighed next to nothing. I was very nearly floating.

And I suddenly felt really generous. I wanted everyone to be as happy as I was, especially Mum. So when I got home, I let myself in and went straight to the kitchen to make her a nice cup of tea. Mum loves tea. But before I had even filled the kettle I overheard Susie talking in the next room.

'You're going to have to tell him sooner or later,' she said.

'I know,' Mum hissed. 'Stop pressuring me. He's only twelve, remember.'

What did she mean, *only* twelve? I am nearly thirteen.

'Tell me what?' I said, coming in to the room (minus the tray of tea I'd planned).

They stared at me in pure horror. I wondered if my flies were undone, but I didn't like to check because I didn't want to draw attention to my downstairs department.

'You need new glasses,' Mum said. 'I'll take you tomorrow.' Then she turned to Susie. 'You see? I can't do this.' She sounded really weird, like her voice was cracking in two.

My stomach tightened and I felt a small snake of ice slither down my spine. Was my eyesight that bad? If I was going blind there wasn't a lot I could do about it, I would just have to be content with some dark glasses and a stick. And maybe even a guide dog. Cool. A Labrador. I hoped it would be black. I prefer black Labradors to the golden ones.

'Tell him,' Susie said, interrupting my plans for going blind.

'I can't,' Mum said in her horrible crackly voice.

She was so upset anyone would think she was the one going blind.

'You have to,' Susie said.

Mum breathed deeply. 'I have to go in to hospital,' she said.

'What kind of hospital?' I asked. Please, please let it not be a top-security mental hospital.

'A hospital hospital,' Mum said, 'with sick people and nurses.'

'Your mum needs to have an operation,' Susie said.

'*Surgery!*' I squawked. 'On your head?'

'My head?' Mum said, looking at me like *I* was the crazy one. She put a hand up to her noggin as if to check it was still there. 'No, not my head,' she said.

'Where?' I said.

'St Mary's,' Mum said.

Susie sighed.

'No, *where*?' I said.

'Umm,' Mum said and looked dumbly at Susie.

'Where on your body?' I said.

'Umm, uh,' Mum said.

'WHERE?'

Mum opened her mouth to speak but only a squeak came out.

Susie and I took a step closer, egging her on. It was like a scene from a crime movie where you are about to hear whodunit just before the victim croaks it.

Mum coughed and closed her eyes. When she opened them again they were all watery. Then she started saying some nonsense words. 'I have a t ... um ... a gro ... er ... umour.'

'You have a rumour?' I said. 'Is it spreading?'

Nobody laughed. That annoyed me, because, face it: that was funny.

'A tumour,' Mum said quickly. 'Like a cyst.'

Susie sighed again.

Mum glowered at her.

'A cyst?' I said to Mum in my best voice of contempt. I'd had a cyst once (on my finger). No way was it this big a deal.

'A cancer tumour,' Mum said. Her voice was this tiny little whisper.

'*A what?*' I choked.

'Don't make me say it again,' Mum said, still in her whispery voice. She sounded like she didn't have enough air to breathe.

'Cancer,' Susie said.

'Who asked you?' I snapped.

Susie was around here far too much these days.

I turned to Mum. 'You can't have cancer,' I said. My voice sounded desperate.

'I know I can't,' Mum said in this deadly quiet voice, 'but I do.'

'But people die of cancer,' I said, and I immediately regretted it because both Mum and Susie started crying.

'Not always. Not nowadays,' Susie said, recovering herself. 'They can fix it now.'

I didn't believe this. 'How do they fix it?' I asked.

Mum took off her glasses and mopped her eyes with a tissue.

'Well, first there is the surgery,' she said, 'then radiotherapy.'

Radiotherapy. I imagined Mum lying in a darkened room listening to Classic FM. I saw her with cucumbers on her eyes and a towel round her head.

'What exactly is radiotherapy?' I asked.

'Radiation therapy,' Susie said. 'They zap the area with X-rays and ...'

'*Radiation*!' I yelled. 'Are you crazy? Radiation killed Dr Who in that Christmas special we watched. Don't you remember? 500,000 Rads of the stuff; just before David Tennant regenerated into Matt Smith.'

'I fell asleep five minutes in,' Mum said.

'And after the radiation, then what? Will you be better then?' I asked.

'I'll probably have to have chemotherapy too,' Mum said.

'*Kee-mo-therapy*!' I squawked. 'What's kee-mo-therapy?'

'Drugs,' Susie said. 'They inject them into your body and it kills the cancer.'

'Cool,' I said. 'Like chemical warfare.'

'Yeah, cool,' Mum said, but she didn't really sound like she meant it. 'There are side effects,' she said. 'You can get really tired.'

'You're already really tired,' I said.

'Well,' Mum said, sounding a bit exasperated, 'I'll be even more tired. And maybe a bit sick.' She turned to Susie. 'The nurse told me that one woman puked into her handbag because she was on a bus and had nowhere else to spew.'

'Ick!' Susie said, then turned to me. 'Quick! Hide all the handbags.'

Suddenly Susie was a comedian. I didn't laugh.

'And,' Mum said, 'my hair might be affected. Bits of it might fall out.'

'What, like *lumps* of it?' I said. 'Won't that look a bit off?'

Mum looked like she was going to cry again.

'Philip, listen to me. My hair will fall out if they give me chemotherapy. All of it.'

'*All* of it?' I said.

This was ridiculous.

'Yes, all of it.'

'What, even your nose hairs?' I said.

She couldn't seriously mean *all* of it.

'Yes, even my nose hairs,' Mum said. The corners of her eyes and mouth drooped down.

'That was supposed to be a joke,' I said. 'Are you serious? Every hair on your body will fall out! You'll be as smooth as an egg?'

'Eggs-actly,' Mum said.

I didn't really think her egg joke was funny but I laughed anyway.

'It'll grow back,' Susie said, 'and it'll be even better than ever.'

'When is it happening?'

'On Tuesday,' Susie said.

'But that's just days away! You can't. It can't …'

Mum didn't speak. Her silence filled the room. It crept into my ears and eyes, into my nose and my throat and suddenly we were crying. All three of us.

I'm not sure why they were crying, but I was crying because I didn't want a baldy mum. Bald was all right for the likes of Harry Hill, but not my mum. When we'd stopped crying I realised she still hadn't told me where the cancer was.

'Where is it?' I asked.

Susie opened her mouth to speak. 'It's …'

'I'm not asking you,' I said through my teeth. 'I'm asking Mum.'

'Breast cancer,' Mum said in a very small voice. 'It's in my …'

'No,' I shouted.

No. No. No. NO! Anything but that. Anything but the B word. How could she do this to me? Now everybody would be saying the word 'breast' all the time as if it were some ordinary everyday word like 'teapot'. Why couldn't she have bowel cancer instead? On second thoughts maybe not. I didn't want people imagining Mum on the loo. Lung cancer, maybe? No, people died of that all the time on TV. What about toe cancer or ear cancer? I could live with that.

Susie broke the silence. 'They remove the breast and ...'

See what I mean. It would be *breast, breast, breast* from there on in. Hang on, did she say remove it? Cut it off!

'Shut up,' I said. 'Shut up. Shut up.'

'Maybe I should go,' Susie said.

'Yeah, maybe you should,' I said, which really wasn't like me.

'Philip!' Mum said. 'Don't be so rude. I want Susie to stay.'

'Suit yourself,' I snapped.

I was fed up with this. I didn't want to think about Mum being sick. I wanted to think about Lucy. And about giving stuff to poor people with her. Instead my head was crammed with images of hospitals with killer X-ray machines and one-boobed, bald-headed women barfing into handbags.

'You've ruined everything,' I said to Mum. 'What am I going to do about Lucy now?'

Mum and Susie stared at each other.

'Who's Lucy?' they said in unison.

Dear Harry Hill

I've been wondering how you went bald. I've always assumed you just shaved your hair off because it looks good for your act, but now I'm not so sure. Did it just fall out with old age or did you take medicine to make it fall out? If it was the medicine, can you please write and tell me what that was like. I've just found out what's wrong with Mum. She has lost her sense of humour because she is going to have to take that medicine too.

No offence, but I think you'll agree that, while it's a good look on you, it's different for women. Can you suggest anything I could do to cheer her up? I know that this is something you can help with because you are bald and funny and you used to be a doctor. Please write back quickly, I'm getting desperate.

Yours sincerely
Philip Wright

14

The Silent Treatment

Have you ever sulked for ages?

And ages.

Jeeeez, it's boring. After Mum had dropped her bombshell, I'd stomped off to my room and lain on my bed playing games on my mobile phone for forever. But then the battery went flat and I couldn't recharge it because that would've involved finding the strength to sit up and reach the plug at the bottom of the bed. Sulking is seriously exhausting; that plug seemed very far away. Boy was I bored! And starving.

Rule number one of sulking: eat first.

I wished Ang had been with me, then I wouldn't have been starving. He never leaves the house without a bar of chocolate in case of emergencies. He is very worried about dropping dead from sudden acute sugar deficiency. If I ever get stuck in a plane crash miles from anywhere, I want Ang to be there too. He'd have loads of sweets to munch on before we'd have to start eating each other's limbs.

The more I thought about Ang and his chocolate-filled pockets, the hungrier I felt. I got up and had a rummage through my cupboards, hoping to find a half-eaten chocolate bar or a packet of crisps, but there was nothing. But I did make one brilliant find – an old pair of specs that I'd forgotten I still had. I loved those specs – they had tiny Scooby Doos on the frames. I'd be able to see again, sort of – the lenses weren't strong enough and they were a bit too small. Well, more than a bit, they felt like a wire coat hanger was clamped to my face, but they'd do for a day or so until Mum brought me spec-shopping. That got me thinking: Do people with cancer actually go shopping? I pictured a supermarket full of people in hospital gowns, miserably pushing trolleys around like zombies in a not very good supermarket-zombie movie.

But I was still hungry. And bored.

If you have any doubt about how bored I was, the next thing I did will convince you: I started thinking about Mrs Gray's poetry – that 'Ode to a Nightingale' one with the sore buttocks, by Keats. And that's when I thought maybe Keats wasn't mad, just bored like me. Let's face it you'd have to be pretty bored to wind up writing poems to birds. Still, a bird friend was better than nothing.

I got up and opened the window but all I could see was an ancient teddy-mauling Chihuahua who was sleeping under the big pine tree that separated our gardens. No birds.

I had a pair of rolled-up socks in my hand, from rummaging around in the drawers, so I took aim and flung the socks at the dog. Don't ask me why. Just because it was there. Like Everest.

The socks landed on the Chihuahua's head. He woke

up and sneezed from the shock, then started attacking the socks with his gums.

I went back to my cupboards and had another rummage for harmless missiles. Revenge had come at last. In the end I decided to stick with rolled-up socks. I didn't want to hurt the mutt, just teach him a lesson, and I only used boring school socks – nobody would miss those.

I'd only been at it for a minute or two when I heard voices outside. Old Mrs Chihuahua was shouting and Susie was saying something I couldn't make out and the next thing I knew, footsteps were thundering up the stairs.

Mum burst in just as I was preparing to fling a three-in-one sock special out the window.

My face boiled.

'Philip,' Mum gasped, 'Mrs Casey says you're attacking her dog. Your socks are all over her lawn.'

I was so flustered, I forgot that I wasn't talking to her.

'How do you know they're mine?' I said, which you have to agree was not clever.

I waited for Mum to start bawling me out. She's not generally a shouter but will rise to the challenge when she has to. But you know what? She didn't. She just sat on my bed and said that old Mrs Chihuahua was downstairs threatening Susie with the police and the RSPCA and Social Services and Help the Aged and the National Lottery and God knows what.

'The lottery?' I said.

'*Joke*, Mr Comedian,' Mum said and kicked off her

shoes. Then she settled herself on top of my bed. 'Are those your old kiddie glasses?'

I touched my hand to the frames. I didn't like her calling them kiddie specs. Scooby Doo appeals to viewers of all ages, doesn't he?

'What were you thinking, you big nitwit?' she said.

'I wasn't.'

'Evidently,' Mum said, closing her eyes and leaning back on my headboard.

It had been a long time since Mum had sat on my bed like that. She used to do it all the time when I was small, to read to me and tell me stories of when she was a child. I loved that. I stared at Mum waiting for her to open her eyes and tell me off. I wished she'd hurry up and get it over with, but she just sat there. I thought maybe she was trying out a new tactic designed to prolong the agony and make me squirm. Well, it worked. I was squirming.

After what felt like hours, but was in fact about five minutes, I couldn't take any more. 'I'm sorry. I shouldn't have done that to Mrs Casey's dog,' I said in my most repentant voice, and I genuinely meant it. I hate that dog for what he did to Sir Fluffington, but I'd never actually harm him. Not that throwing *socks* at the mutt was going to hurt anything other than his dignity. Mum didn't answer.

'Mum?' I said.

She was taking this silent torture thing a bit too far. I waited another few minutes then I leaned over her and poked her gently in the ribs but she didn't even flinch.

'Mum?'

She let out a small snort and her mouth fell open slightly. Fast asleep. Poor old Mum. It must be really exhausting having cancer *and* a crazy, Chihuahua-hating son. She looked lovely lying there; all cosy and sleepy, and not shouting. Her glasses were crooked so I very carefully slipped them off and set them on my bedside table. She looked even nicer then, softer or something. I pulled a blanket up and tucked it round her shoulders then went downstairs to face the music.

15

Lunch Hero

Ang loved the whole Chihuahua-sock saga.

'What did old Mrs Chihuahua do to you?' he asked when I told him the story in the lunch queue the following day. I hadn't told him *why* I'd been hurling socks out my window. We are good friends but I wasn't ready to tell him that my mum would soon be minus one in the boob department.

'She gave me juice and jammy buns with coconut on top,' I said.

'Cool,' Ang said. 'And then did she call the police?' He seemed really keen that I got arrested.

'No,' I said. 'She poured me more juice. I think she felt sorry for me.'

'Why would she feel sorry for you?'

'Dunno, but she kept on saying, "You poor dear," so she must have.'

'So,' Ang said, scratching his head, 'you attack Crazy Dog Woman's pooch with smelly socks and she feeds you buns?'

'They weren't smelly and she's not crazy,' I said. 'She's actually really nice.'

Call me a hypocrite, but I didn't like Ang talking about

old Mrs C like that. And yes, I do know that I was the one who christened her Mrs Chihuahua, but I still didn't like Ang making fun of her. Not now that she'd given me buns.

But Ang wasn't giving up.

'When I first moved here you made me swear to make Mrs Casey and her mutt my mortal enemies.'

'So?'

'So I could have been drinking juice and eating homemade buns instead. Next you'll be telling me she carries the dog around in her handbag and kisses its head, like Paris Hilton and her mutt.'

'Um, she does kiss Alfred Pickles quite a lot,' I said, squirming. 'Wonder what's for lunch today.'

'Who the heck is Alfred Pickles and what's he got to do with anything?'

'That's his name – the dog,' I said, hoping Ang would drop the subject.

I felt rotten because everything Ang knew about Mrs Chihuahua and her dog came from me. But if he'd only seen them together he'd change his mind. Boy, those two are crazy about each other. Mrs Chihuahua let Alfred Pickles climb up on to her lap and lick at her face and slobber all over her. She even took off her slippers and let him lick her feet which was a bit gross – old people have really ugly feet, all gnarled and knobbly like tree roots. Still, it was kind of nice watching the two of them together. They were like best mates or something. It got me thinking that Mum should get a dog. I mean, I'm not going to be around for ever and she'll need something to fill the void when I leave home.

The lunch queue moved half a millimetre forward and then a crowd of fourth-formers came in and bunked in in front of some terrified looking first-years and we were back where we started. I expected Ang to start complaining because he gets a bit ratty when he's hungry but he didn't seem bothered because he just stood there smiling into the distance. I was about to start one of my when-I-rule-the-world speeches (I was planning on life imprisonment for queue-jumpers) when I spotted Lucy and her meerkat friend scanning the crowd for someone.

I craned my neck and stood on my toes. *Here, I'm over here.*

And then, I could not believe my eyes. Right there and then, in full view of everyone, Lucy stopped, took out her purse and handed over its contents.

To The Yeti.

Ang saw it too, but oddly he just kept on smiling like a simpleton.

The Yeti smirked at Lucy and landed his big fat ugly hand on her shoulder. That was it. I clenched my fist and stepped out of the queue. The Yeti was for it this time.

Ang pulled me back. 'You do know you're wearing Scooby Doo glasses, don't you?' he said.

'That big creep is bullying Lucy for her lunch money. She'll be terrified.'

'She doesn't look terrified,' Ang said, and I felt like punching him too.

Of *course* Lucy was scared.

I started after her. And you know what? Ang came too.

He actually left a queue for food and went with me to save Lucy. What a friend!

As soon as we were face to face, Lucy came over all goddessy, giggling and mumbling something to her friend about Scooby Doo, and at that very same moment something happened the wiring in my brain: eighty per cent of my neurotransmitters must have shut down because instead of saying, 'Lucy, are you all right?' only grunts and mangled bits of words came out.

I took off my Scooby Doo specs because I was feeling self-conscious, but then I couldn't see properly and I was squinting at Lucy like a weirdo. Weirdo-squinting stalker is not a good look on me so I put the specs back on.

'Money ... um. Yeti ... um ... lunch ... um,' I said, which in my head translated to 'Lucy, did The Yeti take your lunch money?' but outside my head the words sounded like the chorus of a bizarre and creepy nursery rhyme: 'Money-yum, Yeti-yum, lunch-yum.'

'Smooth-yum,' Ang said and then he coughed this really noisy cough.

Lucy's friend turned to him. She put a hand on his shoulder and said, 'Are you all right? Here, have a sip of my water.' Ang coughed again and took the water bottle she held out to him. He was grinning from ear to ear. Idiot. What was there to grin about?

'Did you want something?' Lucy said.

I stared at her and waited for something that sounded like English to come out of my mouth. 'Yeti ... Was he ...

are you … did he?' I said, which I think you'll agree was about as clear as mud.

'Are you sick or something?' Lucy said.

'Maybe it's code or a rap or something,' the annoying friend said.

And you know what? Ang burst out laughing as if this was the funniest thing he'd ever heard in his entire life.

I shot him a you're-supposed-to-be-my-friend look, but he went on laughing like a hyena. A really stupid hyena that laughs in all the wrong places.

'Did Eddie Lyttle take your money?' I finally managed to say.

Lucy blushed.

She looked down at her feet and her hair fell down over her face. I wanted to reach out and push it back *so* much. But then she whipped back her hair and snapped at me, 'Is that any of your business, Philip Wright?'

That's when I knew I was doomed: girls only call you by your full name when they are truly disgusted with you. And I was right. Lucy told me to stick my nose in somewhere it was wanted, grabbed her friend's arm and stomped off.

Holly, the annoying friend, kept looking back over her shoulder. I think she wanted her water bottle back. But Ang was holding it like it was some kind of prize and he was grinning like a goon. I could have punched him.

Dear Harry Hill

I know you are a busy man but I am beginning to lose patience with you. I have now written to you four times and you haven't written back once.

Things have got a whole lot worse here. Not only do I have Mum to deal with, but I think my bully is now bullying my girlfriend (who isn't really my girlfriend), and my friend Ang (who really is my friend) has started acting weird and has gone off his food.

Can't you see what a terrible mess my life is? Don't you feel anything when a fellow-comedian is suffering? Write back soon. Please.

Yours sincerely
Philip Wright

16

Think Positive

Please don't get the wrong impression when I say that I enjoyed Mum going in to hospital. I know I was supposed to be all freaked out about her operation but the fact is I like hospitals. I can see why Harry Hill thought about becoming a doctor before he became a comedian. For a start, there is all that saving-people's-lives business, and then there is all the cool equipment they have, like drips and monitors and those paddle things they use to shock people back to life.

The truth is, Mum going in to hospital was kind of exciting, and I think she thought it was exciting too because she was buzzing the day before the operation. When I came home from school she was furiously cleaning the house again. She was 'putting things in order' she said. Anybody would've thought they were going to perform her surgery on the kitchen table the way she kept scrubbing at it. Since being diagnosed with cancer Mum had become a complete clean freak. She was cleaning the house like her life depended on it, like she was trying to control all the germs in the world and tell them where to go. I could have told her she was wasting her time because cancer isn't caused by germs; it's caused by out-of-control cell growth. I know this because I read it on the internet, but I didn't tell Mum because I didn't want to burst her bubble. I just followed her around and told her loads of old jokes to keep her company while she cleaned.

And then (I do feel a tiny bit guilty about this) on the actual day of the operation Susie let me stay off school *and* she said we could go shopping for new specs – and I can't pretend I wasn't pleased about the school part because I am only human.

Susie said we should make a day of it, have lunch out and everything. I didn't see how buying specs could take a whole day but I went along with it anyway. I was right, I found the pair of frames I wanted straight away. But Susie said no. She said Mum would have two hernias and rip her stitches open if we didn't come back with something *sensible*. I think what she really meant was boring. Instead of taking the specs I wanted (big black frames like Harry Hill's) we spent so much time in the optician's that I was beginning to think blind people had it easy. They didn't have to go through all that malarkey: put on the grey ones; take them off; put on the silver ones; take them off; no, no, put them on again; no, put the grey ones back on; no, not *those* grey ones, *those ones*. After about an hour of that, I felt like gouging my own eyes out with a rusty spoon and saving us all a whole heap of bother.

Did I tell you that I hate shopping? And after three hours in a shop with me, so did Susie.

'Never again,' she said, flopping down into a seat in the café next to the optician's.

I don't think Susie genuinely hated being out with me, it was just that she was really worried about Mum. She kept biting her nails and saying stuff like, 'She'll have had her pre-med by now.' 'She'll be in recovery now.' 'She'll ...'

Honestly, adults are impossible. Someone should tell them that it is not a good tactic to keep talking about what is worrying you. It only makes matters worse.

And the thing is I wasn't really worried. Mum had told me that everything was going to be all right and I believed her. Mum is *the* person in my life; the one who is just always there, doing stuff, getting on my nerves, knowing everything. I literally couldn't begin to think of anything bad happening to her. When I tried, my mind just went blank like a faulty computer screen.

And if you really want to know the truth, I was more worried about Mrs Gray's poetry session, which was lined up for the very next day. Why did I ever tell her that I was a poet? I am *so* not poet material. Poets are all tragic and sad and die at an early age. I am comic and happy and plan to live way in to my nineties. Not to mention the minor detail that I cannot actually write poetry. And I had to come up with volume one for my personal poetry session in less than twenty-four hours.

You know how you hear writers on the TV talking about writing? (I say writers, but I've only ever heard one, on *Blue Peter*.) Well, he said you should write about yourself or something you know. Generally, I think that is rubbish advice because most people just know about getting up and going to school or work then coming home and having their tea. Who wants to read about that? I like reading adventure/crime/action/sci-fi novels and I don't for one minute believe my favourite writers have garrotted a Russian spy with cheese wire, hung upside down from a flag pole over a busy London street or travelled to Mars. So I am taking that piece of advice with a pinch of salt. However, it did get me thinking about myself and my predicament, or rather Mum's, and I had this brilliant idea that maybe I could write a poem about that.

Oh boob, goodbye
Oh boob, farewell,
Oh mother, do not cry,
With that big woolly jacket on,
No-one could ever tell.

On second thoughts, maybe not.

'Are you any good at writing poems?' I asked Susie.

'What? Poems?' she said, gnawing away at her fingernails. She took her hand out of her mouth. 'Do you think we could go and see her?'

'Are you mad?' I said. 'I've only got one poem written so far.'

'What?' Susie said and went on gnawing her fist.

'Oh, *Mum*, of course,' I said, trying to push all thoughts of poetry out of my head. 'They told us we can't visit Mum until after three, remember?'

'I know, but …' Susie said chewing her nails some more. Her self-cannibalism was starting to freak me out so I decided to distract her with a joke.

Patient: Doctor, doctor, every time I drink a cup of tea I get a stabbing pain in my eye.

Doctor: Try taking the spoon out first.

It worked! Susie laughed so much she nearly swallowed her own fist.

'You are a tonic, Philip,' she said. 'With you around your mum can't go wrong. You know, they say your chances of getting better increase if you are positive and cheerful. It's called PMA, Positive Mental Attitude.'

'You mean jokes are actually medically good for you? Cool!'

Maybe I could visit sick people and see if they got better after my performances. Wow! Think about it: I could become a world-famous healing comedian who helps sick people find health and long life. A bit like Jesus, but with a sense of humour.

I was seriously excited about this whole PMA thing and I decided to write to Harry Hill about it. I agonised about whether or not to apologise for telling him I was cross with him in my last letter, but in the end I decided not to. I might end up making matters worse. I couldn't risk upsetting Harry Hill. With Mum sick, I needed him more than ever.

Dear Harry Hill

Have you heard of PMA? It stands for Positive Mental Attitude. It is amazing; apparently, sick people can make themselves better if they stay positive and happy. I know it sounds a bit far-fetched, but I thought you might know something about it. And if you don't, I could look into it for you.

I will make sure I keep mum positive and happy and see what effect it has on her health and then I'll let you know what happens. Deal?

Yours sincerely

Philip Wright

PS: If this PMA thing is true, think of the possibilities. It could be the medical breakthrough of the century. We could become famous and rich and Mum would be cured.

(It occurred to me that Harry Hill was already famous and rich but I left that bit in anyway.)

17
Homecoming

I didn't show Mum my new glasses for a few days because I was a bit nervous that she would freak out and shout and do herself an injury when she saw that they were Harry Hill glasses. But you know what? When I finally walked in wearing them she just said, 'Crikey, *You've been framed*,' which was quite clever for a sick person, don't you think?

'Don't worry,' Susie said. 'It was buy-one-get-one-free, so he does have sensible ones too. But for now the look is geek chic!'

'Geek freak,' Mum said. And the two of them had a good old giggle. I had made Mum laugh and I hadn't even said a word. If there really was anything in this PMA lark, Mum would be cured in no time.

Then a doctor came round and spoiled it all.

He told Mum she could go home the following day, and you know what she did? She burst into tears. It just goes to show you that you cannot trust an adult. There she was saying how much she hated hospital and complaining about how boring it was and how it *smelled,* and how she wanted home to be with me, but all the time she was secretly glad to be there. Like I said, I could see the attraction of hospital, but one week was enough. It was time for Mum to come home. And I can tell you, I was not impressed to hear she didn't feel the same.

Not only did she not want to be home with me, but she preferred the company of snoring, groaning (her words) strangers. I just couldn't fathom it. And what was the doctor going to think of me? He'd probably think I was some kind of tearaway that Mum was trying to escape. You know, like the kind you see on Channel Four shockumentaries: 'I had my vital organs removed to get away from my delinquent son.'

I could see the doctor wasn't impressed with either of us because he didn't let Mum stay. She kept on sobbing that she wasn't ready and that she couldn't cope, but he just looked at her like she was speaking Ancient Greek. It really was an impressive display of heartlessness. I felt a bit in awe of him. And it served Mum right for not wanting to come back to me.

She came home the next day, and there followed the worst few weeks of my life. Mum was impossible. She slept a lot and cried a lot and drank a lot of tea. Once when I brought her a cup of tea (in her favourite cup) she said it was the wrong colour and burst into tears. Having your boob chopped off must make you colour-blind because there was nothing wrong with the colour of that tea. And there was nothing wrong with the taste of it either. I know because I took a sip of it to check it was just right before I brought it to her. Just goes to show the thanks you get.

I felt like crying over that tea myself but I'm not that

childish, and anyway I didn't have time. I had a million things to do, like putting on the washing and taking out the washing and hanging up the washing, then taking it down again and folding it and putting it away. I didn't have to do the ironing because Mum thinks me and a hot iron are a dangerous combination. What an insult, but I didn't argue – I was doing plenty as it was. Honestly, all that laundry was enough to make you want to wear the same pair of socks for a week. We could all be a lot more economical with our clothes-wearing. It just isn't worth it.

Eventually, Mum did get up and about and started doing things around the house but she didn't return to her fanatical pre-operation cleaning frenzy. In fact, the house started to look a bit of a mess. Obviously, things being in order didn't matter any more.

Dear Harry Hill

I am sorry for saying I was losing patience with you. I know how busy and exhausted you must be watching TV all day, so I am really sorry. Anyway, you won't have to put up with me for much longer.

Mum has had an operation, sort of like an amputation but I don't want to say what bit they chopped off. Anyway, she needs me to do a million things for her, so assuming I don't die of exhaustion, I won't have time to write for a while.

And if I do find any time for writing, I'll be frantically scribbling poems because my English teacher is still waiting to hear my poetry. So if you don't hear from me it's just because I am busy or have stabbed myself with my own poetry-hating pen and not because of any ill feeling.

Please forgive me. I am still your number one fan.

Philip Wright

18

The Midas Touch – *Not*

After a few weeks of lolling around doing nothing and getting cups of tea brought to her, Mum went back to the hospital for the next stage. Instead of making Mum better, the doctors actually made her sicker. They call it 'treatment', apparently.

Poor Mum. When she wasn't sleeping, she was vomiting, and when she wasn't sleeping or vomiting, she was crying and worrying and demanding cups of tea and then not drinking them. Poor Mum. Poor me. She kept apologising for not being fun any more, which was very thoughtful of her.

To begin with I just said, 'Don't be silly, Mum, you're sick; no one expects you to be fun.' But as time wore on I got a bit fed up with it and I did wonder if maybe she could make a tiny bit more effort to jazz herself up.

And as if all that wasn't enough, the bad things weren't confined to Mum being sick. Cancer was a cancer on my life. (I think that is a metaphor.), Everything I put my hand to turned to disaster. I was like that King Midas with the weird curse where everything he touched turned to gold, except that the things I touched didn't turn to gold; they turned to a big heap of stinking rot. Did you know that if you rearrange the letters of Midas it spells 'I'm sad'? Freak-ee or what! Because, believe me, I *was* sad. And I know you'll agree that I had good cause to be when you hear my long list of bad things. Be warned: this involves the word *breast*.

BAD THING NUMBER *ONE:* I said the word breast to Mrs Gray the English teacher.
BAD THING NUMBER *TWO:* I think Ang is in love with Lucy.
BAD THING NUMBER *THREE:* I think Lucy is in love with Ang.
BAD THING NUMBER *FOUR:* All Mum's hair fell out.

And that list doesn't even mention the poetry problem. Mrs Gray kept on at me for weeks about it, and that's how Bad Thing Number One came about.

I'd managed to give Mrs Gray's poetry session the slip several times by getting myself lunchtime detentions for coughing in RE class. Miss Box, the RE teacher (that really is her name) dislikes coughing. She dislikes noises of any kind and prefers us to work in complete silence. I think she has some kind of noise-induced persecution complex because she thinks we are always out to trick her and make fun of her. Actually, come to think of it, we are, but only because we will die of boredom otherwise. Anyway, I did start deliberately annoying Miss Box because she loves lunchtime detentions and that meant I could escape the one-on-one lunchtime English treat that was lined up for me.

But Mrs Gray caught up with me in the end.

She nabbed me one day as I was trying to scuttle out of her classroom at Friday home time. 'Philip Wright,' she said, 'you've let me down. I waited for you at lunchtime three Wednesdays in a row and you didn't show.'

Is red the colour of guilt? If so, my ears were as guilty as hell. They were on fire.

'You didn't even bother to explain why,' Mrs Gray went on.

Ang once told me that when you are in trouble you should say nothing, and since I had nothing to say for myself I decided to take his advice. But it only seemed to rattle Mrs Gray more. She stared at me and waited for me to respond. When I didn't, she said, 'I'm very disappointed in you, Philip.'

Aww, now why did she have to go and say that? I hate disappointing people. I hate them thinking I'm a no good lousy louse. Even when I am. I hated disappointing her so much that I opened my mouth right there and then and said, 'Why don't we do it now?'

You know how people say 'the silence was deafening' and you think that's stupid because silence isn't deafening, it's silent? Well, when you've sat across the table from your English teacher *not* discussing poetry you'll know what they mean. Mrs Gray bombarded me with a tonne of questions about Wordsworth and the other poets and I just sat there deafening her with my silence. A silence so pure you could hear the molecules in the air move. They made a kind of thumping noise in my head, like a pulse. It got louder with every second that passed.

'Did the subject matter interest you?' Mrs Gray probed.

I stared at the table. Fascinating things, tables. Most people don't take the time to fully appreciate the table. And I don't just mean its construction and design; if you look closely at its surface you can see tiny scratches and pock marks and stains. There was even a burn mark on this table where Pete 'Gingernut' McKenna had tried to set fire to our test papers last summer. He got suspended and we had to take the test again so it was a lose–lose outcome for everyone, but at least you could say there was history in that table.

Mrs Gray coughed. 'Philip? What about your own poetry then, since my lot didn't do it for you?'

And you know what? I was actually relieved. At least I knew what *my* Lucy poem was about. I took a crumpled page from my pocket and set it on top of Pete McKenna's scorch mark.

Oddly, Mrs Gray didn't seem that impressed with it. A small crease appeared in her forehead as she read; then she folded the page over and said, 'Any more?'

'Not quite,' I said, which I thought sounded open-ended enough to keep her happy, but I was wrong – the look of disappointment on her face would have broken a monster.

'But I'm working on a new one,' I said, trying to un-disappoint her.

'Oh?' she said, brightening a bit. 'Let's have it.'

I stared at her. I stared at the table. I stared at the floor. Mrs Gray tried to help me along with an encouraging smile. It was more like the kind of smile you'd give a toddler than an almost-teenager, kind of like the aren't-you-a-cute-puppy smiles Ang's mum gives me. Hey! That was it! Thank you, Ang's mum.

I opened my mouth and said in this really dramatic voice, 'Where there is love, there is pain.'

Mrs Gray looked impressed. She smiled at me and nodded. I closed my eyes and pressed my fingers to my temples and massaged the skin there to try and make it look like I was being really creative and thoughtful. 'Where there is light, there is dark,' I said. 'Where there is silence, there is noise.'

I was impressed. This poetry lark was a breeze; all you had to do was throw some random words together and make sure they all bounced along nicely. I was feeling quite pleased with myself and opened my mouth ready to let my poetic genius pour forth.

'Where there is ...'

I stalled.

I started again. 'Where there is ...'

I stalled again.

I sat there opening and closing my mouth but no sound came out.

I was like a goldfish drowning out of water. And yes, I do know what that looks like because in nursery school Jimmy Palmer took the class goldfish out of its tank so that it could play with us in the sand pit. It didn't like playing in the sand. It died. But not before it had opened and closed its mouth at us, silently crying out for help.

I was that fish.

You know how they say a drowning man's life flashes before him? Well, that's what happened to me. Except it was worse for me because presumably the drowning man didn't have his English teacher breathing down his neck. Well, all the things that had been worrying me crowded into my brain at once: The Yeti, Mum, Harry Hill, Mum, The Goddess, Mum, Ang, Mum, Poor people, Mum, Chihuahuas, Mum. Can you see a pattern beginning to emerge here? It doesn't take a genius to figure out that I was more worried about Mum than I'd realised. Or maybe it does. Maybe I could be a genius psychologist when I grow up and tell people what is worrying them.

'Philip, are you all right?' Mrs Gray said.

That's when I realised there were tears starting at the corners of my eyes.

OH MY GOD. STOP. CANNOT CRY IN FRONT OF TEACHER.

'Philip?' she said again in this weird and velvety voice that sounded like a real person, not a teacher. 'Would you like to talk about it?'

'Mum,' I squeaked and blinked away my tears.

'Ahh,' Mrs Gray said.

'Sick,' I squeaked.

'Mmm,' she said soothingly.

'Breast,' I whispered.

'Hmm?' she said.

'Breast,' I said a bit louder. I couldn't get the 'cancer' bit out; it seemed to have lodged at the back of my throat. I tried again.

'Breast,' I squawked.

And that was the end of Velvety Voice. Mrs Gray's face was the colour of boiled beetroot. She shot up out of her chair and backed away from me, buttoning her blouse up to the neck.

Oh my God! Did she think I meant *her* breast?

OH. MY. GOD. Beam me up. NOW!

19

Secrets and Lies

I ran out of school and all the way home. I couldn't wait to tell Ang the whole thing. We hadn't exactly been seeing eye to eye recently and Mrs Gray's boobs could be just the thing to bring us back together.

Part of the problem was that I was being so secretive. I still hadn't said anything to him about Mum. How could I: 'Hey, Ang. You know my mum's breasts? Well, she's only got one.' What if he laughed? Or worse, what if he went all quiet and doom-struck?

One of the problems with being secretive is that it's contagious. Ever since I'd started holding back from Ang, he'd started holding back from me. He said I was acting weird but really I reckon it was him. When I called for him, he said he was busy – Facebooking somebody. What kind of friend does that? I was his friend with my face right there on his doorstep; he didn't need some nobody from cyberspace. And nearly every time I phoned him I got an engaged tone. Why would he spend all that time talking to someone who wasn't me? I know I wasn't my usual fun-loving self, and OK, I do admit that sometimes I avoided him in case the conversation came round to Mum, but still.

Some days I couldn't even find him at lunch break. Normally we just meet up. It's not an arrangement or anything, it just kind of happens, but last week he wasn't in his usual spot by the vending machines. (His sweet tooth extends to all and any soft drinks.) Twice I've had to go and track him down. Today I spotted him heading into the library. I thought maybe he was sick because who goes to the library at lunchtime? So I followed him. I will never forget what I saw: Ang was sitting there like Lord Chuffin' Muck all cosied up with Lucy and her friend Holly the Meerkat.

They were poring over books and whispering to each other. Lucy's head was so close to his, and their hands were almost touching, and The Meerkat was giggling away like an idiot. It was enough to make a grown boy cry.

I tried to stay angry at Ang but even though he was a low-down, love-rat creep, he was still my friend and I couldn't imagine not hanging out with him. Anyway, I'd given him the cold shoulder all afternoon so I reckoned he'd been punished enough. I made up my mind to find him, tell him about Mum and reduce him to a quivering wreck of laughter with my Mrs Gray's boobs story. And I wouldn't wait; I'd do it right there and then.

But before I got to his house, I saw him step out his front door. He'd changed out of his school uniform and was wearing enough hair gel to wallpaper a room. He waved to someone on the other side of the street then crossed over to meet them.

The other person was waving back. And smiling. It was Lucy.

I stood there speechless. Lucy's annoying friend Holly the Meerkat was there too. She was waving and giggling and generally being her usual annoying self. They were all so wrapped up in each other they didn't even see me. They just turned and walked away together. All three of them.

Naturally, I followed them. What else could I do?

I tailed them at a safe distance. There could always be some perfectly innocent explanation for all of this. Maybe Lucy was helping Ang with his homework. The trouble was, there were no schoolbags but there was lots of giggling coming from the girls, and Ang was grinning like a chimpanzee with lockjaw. I followed them to the park and when they stopped at the swings I had to duck behind a tree in case they spotted me.

Then I saw a fourth person coming to join them. Lucy waved and beckoned him over. It was Hoodie Guy. What was going on? Was Lucy two-timing Ang with that hoodie creep? Serve him right if she was. He knew I loved Lucy. Hoodie Guy moved in really close to Lucy and said something. Then he turned to Holly and said something that must have been *hil*-arious because they all burst out laughing and she started poking him in the ribs with her stupid fingers. And before you could say 'What are you doing, you pack of low-down treacherous traitors?' they were all horse-playing around and Holly reached up and pulled the guy's hood down and he ...

Oh My God! It was The Yeti.

I felt like I had been stabbed in the heart. How could Lucy? How could Ang? I noticed a warm wet feeling on my leg and wondered if my metaphorical stab wound had somehow started bleeding out my shins. I've always liked the idea of being a medical freak but right then was not the time. Still, I was a bit disappointed when I looked down and did not see actual blood stains. I saw dog pee. A nice fresh torrent of the stuff with steam coming off. Alfred Pickles was looking up at me with his great big Chihuahua eyes and peeing on my leg as if it was the most natural thing in the world.

He was out for a walk with old Mrs Chihuahua and she'd let him off his lead – to 'go pee-pees' and then she'd lost track of him.

'Alfred,' she called. 'Pickly-Wickly, where are you?'

I tried to shoo the dog away from me. The last thing a spy needs is a dotty old lady and an incontinent dog giving the game away. By the time Mrs Casey found us, *Pickly Wickly* had emptied the entire contents of his bladder onto my leg. Then he decided he wanted the contents back. He grabbed hold of my trouser leg and was shaking his head frantically from side to side and growling and backing away from me, all at the same time.

Can dogs be mentally unstable? If so, Alfred 'Pickly-Wickly' Pickles was definitely nuts.

'Naughty, naughty,' Mrs Casey crooned, stooping to pick up the dog.

You'd think a tiny old woman like Mrs Casey would have a tiny old woman voice, wouldn't you? Well, you'd be wrong. She was crowing away at the top of her lungs. How was I going to spy on Ang with her making all that racket? James Bond never had this problem. I bent down to try and shush her up and help get her lunatic dog off me – Alfred Pickles had seriously strong jaws for a geriatric pooch. When finally we freed my trouser leg from his mouth, I stood up to see four faces staring at me.

Yes, you've guessed it: Lucy, Ang, Holly and The Yeti.

'Have you wet yourself?' The Yeti asked.

'Yeah, because I pee out my kneecaps,' I said, trying to sound cool and condescending but I'm pretty sure my boiled red face was a dead giveaway that I was squirming.

'Your kneecaps?' The Yeti said, as if he actually believed that could happen.

Ang let out a laugh but he shut up when Holly the Meerkat shoved her elbow into him.

'Don't listen to him, Eddie,' The Goddess said, 'he thinks he's clever.'

'Yeah, you're right, Luce,' The Yeti said, turning away.

Luce!

'Such a naughty boy!' Mrs Casey said, smothering the dog with her face.

Now, I don't care what anybody says. It was obvious that Mrs Casey was talking to Pickly flippin' Wickly and not me. Any idiot could have seen that. But you know what they all did – yeah, that's right. They all fell about laughing. Ang most of all – he kept trying to catch my eye, like we were mates or something. Like this was actually funny.

'We're going to be late,' Holly the Meerkat said.

'We're going down to the …' Ang started, but Lucy cut across him.

'Philip can't come – he'll stink of dog pee!'

Then Mrs Casey said, 'We'd need to be getting home, mister. It's way past your bed time.' And they all fell about laughing again.

OK, I am going to say this one more time – she was talking to the dog, do you hear me, *THE DOG!*

As the others started to leave, Ang turned to me. He looked like he was going to say something but then that seriously annoying meerkat Holly nudged him and he just shrugged and moved off. Traitor.

20
ASS

I'm not going to lie to you; what Ang did really hurt. I stopped speaking to him after that and even though he came up to me a few times at school I just blanked him. Even when he tried to get round me with a joke.

One day he had the nerve to walk right up to me and ask, 'How does the man in the moon cut his hair?' And you know what I did? I just turned and walked away, as if Ang was invisible. I didn't even bat an eyelid, not even when he shouted after me, 'E-clipse it.'

It was really satisfying ignoring Ang like that. For about half a minute. Then it was just lonely and miserable. When Mum first started acting weird I looked forward to school as a refuge, but then Ang and Lucy and The Yeti started acting weird and school was an extra little slice of hell. And we were actually expected to do some work, you know. Teachers kept telling me my work was slipping or that I wasn't trying. They kept overusing the word 'potential'. Apparently I have it. You tell me – how is a boy with potential supposed to work when his whole life is in a downward spiral of downwardness?

Everything was bad. Friends were bad, school was bad and home was bad. It was unbearable. It can't be good for you to be in a constant state of misery like that. In fact I can prove it's not good for you because I developed a new condition: Accumulated Stress Syndrome. I diagnosed myself because Mum didn't have time to take me to the doctor. And anyway I didn't want to burden her. Accumulated Stress Syndrome – ASS to you and me – occurs when stress keeps building up day by day until you feel you can't take the weight of it any more and your skin erupts in a hideous rash of acne as if to say enough is enough.

But the stress just kept coming – Mum's weirdness had reached new heights. The other day she yelled at me because I put a spoon in the fork section of the cutlery drawer (I am not making this up), and then when I said, 'So what?' she took the spoon out and threw it at me! Seriously, she threw it right at me. It missed, but that's not the point: Mum had finally gone completely barking mad. And then you know what she did? She started bawling her eyes out, which was seriously unfair because I should have been the one crying, not her. Luckily, Susie was there at the time to referee. She says Mum's weirdness is due to a combination of stress and medication, but I think that is just plain daft. You'd think being stressed out about cancer would make you appreciate life more, make you love people (me) more, not go around shrieking and hurling spoons about.

Shortly after the spoon incident, Ang called to the house. I opened the door and stared at him. I felt like saying, 'Come right on in, you stinking cheating love rat.

Bring your new girlfriend Lucy, bring your new best friend Yetiman. Come and see my marvellous life with my falling grades and my unrequited love and my one-boobed, bald-headed mother who throws cutlery at me.'

Instead I said, 'What do you want?'

'Nothin',' Ang said.

'Right,' I said and closed the door.

Half an hour later he texted me and asked me what I was doing. I deleted the text.

Dear Harry Hill
I know you're not interested in medicine any more but would you happen to know any cures for acne? My face is so spotty and lumpy, the geography teacher could use it as a 3D relief map of the Rocky Mountains. It's my ASS causing it.

Yours sincerely
Philip Wright

PS I want my friend Ang back. Any ideas?

21
Pillow Talk

It was ten o'clock on a Sunday morning when it happened. I remember the time exactly because I could hear the radio from Mum's bedroom. The ten o'clock news bulletin had just ended when I heard a scream. I stood outside her door for a moment, terrified. I hoped I hadn't made a mistake when I was putting the laundry away the previous day. One stray sock in her knicker drawer was enough to push her over the edge these days. I heard a choking sound and decided there was nothing else for it: I would have to go in.

I found Mum staring at her pillow with a stricken face. I stared at the pillow too because I thought, *Oh here we go, now Mum has developed a fear of untidy pillows*, but then I saw it – a small furry animal lying on her pillow, only it wasn't a small furry animal, it was Mum's hair lying there, without her. Mum was holding on to her head with both hands as if she was trying to stop the rest of her hair falling out which was really very silly and very sad at the same time.

She didn't speak to me and I didn't speak to her. I just stood beside her and put my hand on her arm and began slowly stroking it. We stayed like that for ages. I honestly have no idea who I was comforting, her or me. Both I suppose.

Then I walked over to the phone and dialled Susie's number. I didn't tell her what the problem was, but she knew from the sound of my voice that it was something big. How do you tell someone over the phone that your mum is going bald? Impossible. Impossible and ridiculous and insane and cruel and bloody well unfair. Yes bloody. Bloody bloody bloody. I don't care who hears me swear now. This was so bloody well not fair.

Susie came round straight away. I think she'd guessed what the problem was because she was already crying when I opened the door. When I brought her upstairs, Mum was still standing there staring at the pillow. Susie asked me if I wanted to go round to Ang's house but Mum said softly, 'No, let him stay.'

You have no idea how good that made me feel. Mum had been so irritable with me all the time. I'd heard Susie say that stress can be a cause of cancer and I felt *so* guilty. I was always stressing Mum out – getting detentions, breaking my specs, messing up the cutlery drawer. Sometimes I felt like the cancer was all my fault.

Mum seemed to know what I was thinking. She gave me a hug.

Then Susie said, 'Ready?'

Mum nodded and I stepped back to let them through the door and watched as they locked themselves in the bathroom.

I had no idea what to do then, so I just sat down at the

top of the stairs outside the bathroom and waited. I heard a buzzing sound coming from the room and I thought, *I will never understand women.* All they could think to do at a time like that was brush their teeth. Together. (You have got to admit that that is weird.)

When they didn't stop after the two minutes cleaning Mum always insists upon I called out, 'What's with the marathon tooth-brushing session?'

But they just ignored me and went on brushing for ages. And ages. While I waited outside on tenterhooks. I have no idea what tenterhooks are (or is that ten*der*hooks?), but anyway, I have heard the word used in that kind of way many times and I like the sound of it, don't you? I'll look it up some time when this is all over.

It turned out that the sound I heard wasn't an electric toothbrush duet; it was Mum's electric leg razor. Susie had used it to shave off what was left of Mum's hair. She came out of the bathroom and poked a finger behind her glasses to wipe away a stray tear. I told her she didn't look too bad, but honestly, she looked awful. She smiled nervously at me and I smiled back hoping she couldn't tell what I was thinking.

Then Susie said we all deserved a big Sunday fry-up and led Mum down the stairs. When they'd gone I went into the bathroom and locked the door. It was my turn for a cry.

Dear Harry Hill

I hope I'm not disturbing you from getting ready for your new (can't wait) TV series; ironing those enormous shirt collars must be really time-consuming. But I just had to write.

It has finally happened. And it is every bit as bad as Mum said it would be. The chemotherapy drugs have made all Mum's hair fall out and she doesn't look like Mum any more. She looks like you. I didn't want to tell you the details of Mum's illness, but I suppose the chemotherapy is a bit of a give away. So now you know.

Yours sincerely

Philip Wright

PS: I'm beginning to think PMA isn't all it's cracked up to be, so don't make any firm plans yet about a career in healthcare entertainment.

22

Desperate Measures

Mum stopped going out. I'm serious – she stayed in the house all day, every day and, as far as I could tell, did absolutely nothing. *Nothing.* The house would be a mess when I'd get back from school and the curtains would still be drawn and you can bet your life savings that if she'd still had hair, it would definitely not have been combed.

Sometimes she would be back in bed with a mess of cups and plates and tissues around her. She even started shopping online just so as she wouldn't have to leave the house. The only time she went out was to attend one of her hospital appointments and then she wrapped herself up in so many layers (wig and scarf and hat) you'd have trouble identifying her in a line-up. I think that was the point.

But it was pointless because you could tell something was up. Even old Mrs Chihuahua noticed, and I think she is half blind. She very kindly started bringing round flasks of old-lady soup which were surprisingly yummy and did not taste of boiled knitting as you might expect. I tried to get Mum to answer the door and take the flasks from Mrs C but she wouldn't budge.

I was beginning to fear that Mum was turning into one

of those crazies you hear about who do not leave the house for decades and who collect used bottle tops and empty crisp packets for a hobby. (I saw a documentary about this one time, so I know what I am talking about.) Then one day Mum refused to even go into the back garden and I knew we were just one step away from becoming a documentary ourselves: The woman who stays in bed all day and her son who has to do EVERYTHING.

That's when I knew I had to get Susie involved. *More* involved that is. She came round straight away. Susie is very dependable like that. Mum should think herself lucky. Some of us would kill to have a friend like that. (Ang and I still weren't talking.) She came breezing into the house, barking orders and being very un-Susie-like. She pulled back curtains and opened windows and lifted a series of half empty tea cups from around the place. She found two sitting on the window sill.

'Thinking of starting a penicillin factory?' she said and thrust the mugs at me, as if this was all my fault.

I stared into the mugs. The surface of the liquid was covered in an impressive lumpy blue mould. Cool.

'Go on then, wash,' Susie barked.

I hid one of the mugs in the cupboard under the sink. No point in chucking out perfectly good mould.

When I'd finished washing up, Susie handed me the hoover and said, 'Go on. Clean. You live here too, you know.'

Oh, thank you for that revelation, I wanted to say to her, *because I had no idea where I lived*. But I didn't because

Susie (bossy or not) was the best chance Mum and I had. But I did hope she'd go a bit easier on Mum, because I didn't think she was up to being barked at. I needn't have worried.

'Let's go for a quick walk round the block,' she said gently to Mum, 'just to get a bit of air.'

'I can't,' Mum said.

'Yes you can,' Susie said. 'I'll come with you.'

'I can't,' Mum said again.

Then she pulled off her bandana and sat there with her bald head. (She could hardly sit there without it, but you know what I mean.)

Nobody said anything.

'Can I come too?' I said, just to break the silence. Everyone ignored me, but I didn't let it bother me. I get that a lot. I just said, 'We could go to the park.'

'I am not going out,' Mum said. 'How can I?' Her voice sounded like she didn't have enough air to speak. 'Look at me. *Look!*'

She rolled her bandana into a ball and threw it at Susie. Then she just sat there sobbing and howling and Susie told her to go ahead and let it all out. To tell you the truth I didn't think it would do Mum any harm to keep some of it in. All that emotion was wearing her out. And me.

Have you ever seen *Jurassic Park*? Remember the noise *Tyrannosaurus rex* makes when it gets injured, just before it dies? Well, the noise my mum made that day seriously resembled the cry of a dying dinosaur. She could get a job as a dinosaur voice-double any day. Impressive. And scary.

Susie went over and sat beside her and tried to convince her that things weren't so bad, but Mum wasn't listening.

'I am not going out. People will see. People will know,' she sobbed.

'Is that so bad?' Susie said. When Mum didn't answer, Susie lifted the holdall she'd brought with her and said, 'All right then, if you won't go out, we'll stay in.' And she pulled out her pyjamas and a bottle of wine. 'Wine sleepover,' she announced.

'Have you forgotten?' Mum said. 'I can't drink.'

'No, but I can,' Susie said with a laugh. 'You can watch. Just like the old days when you were pregnant with Junior here.'

'This isn't the old days,' Mum said in this depressingly depressing voice.

So much for PMA, I thought, and left them to it.

I went upstairs and locked myself in the bathroom. I didn't have to go to the toilet. I just wanted to be in a room where no-one could come barging in and tell me to do something. I sat on the loo (seat down, trousers up) and racked my brains trying to think what I could do to help.

The phrase 'Desperate times call for desperate measures' kept swimming around in my head. Our history teacher, Mr Ross, had been overusing the phrase a lot in reference to our poor marks. He claims it originates from Guy Fawkes, but I think he is just making that up because what is the point of a desperate measure that is more desperate than the desperate problem? Guy Fawkes ended up dead, you know, minus his … head. And that is when I came up with my amazingly brilliant, incredibly genius (and a little bit scary) idea.

I stood in front of the bathroom mirror and braced myself. The pink plastic felt sweaty in my hand. I pressed the on switch and the razor buzzed into life. I touched it to my head and instantly recoiled. It was deafening. But I had to do this. There was nothing else for it, so I clenched my teeth and eyes really tight and put the screaming razor to my head again. Then I realised I had my eyes closed. A boy could lose an ear that way.

When I saw that the first glide had not left me bloodied and dying, I knew I could do it. It took ages. Even though my hair is really short, I kept having to stop and clear out clogged-up hair from the blades. I used the same tactic I use when Mum makes me cut the grass: I went round twice, making sure I'd got all the stray bits and had a good smooth finish. The result wasn't exactly what I'd been aiming for. I looked a bit deranged, a cross between a slow loris and a psycho killer, because my eyes seemed bigger than usual, over-sized, like they didn't fit my face any more.

I stared at the scary bald kid in the mirror. He stared back at me.

'Here's to you, Harry Hill,' he said. 'This better work.'

Then I slipped into my room, pulled on a woolly hat and climbed into bed.

Dear Harry Hill

I'm sorry I haven't written in ages. Being miserable is very time-consuming, you know. Anyway, I'm just writing to let you know that I've shaved my head too and with my new glasses on I look like a mini you! Cool or what?

Yours sincerely

Philip Wright

PS: Could you let me know where you buy those big collars you wear?

23

My Life Is Not an Action Movie

The morning after I'd shaved my head, I got up early and left for school before Mum was even out of bed. I slipped out of the house leaving her a note saying I had early games practice and had to be in school before eight. I had to get out; I couldn't risk her seeing me. Not yet.

'You look weird,' Ang said to me as I grabbed some books from my locker. I wondered if he meant woolly-hat-weird or bald-under-your-woolly-hat-weird but I didn't stop to ask him.

It was nearly break time before I was made to take the hat off. Wearing hats in class is forbidden, apparently. So is wearing no hair. We were in art at the time. Miss Franks said, 'What's with the tea-cosy, Philip?' and everyone had a laugh at my expense, but I didn't care. I had to do this. I guess Miss Franks thought that her tea-cosy joke would make me take my hat off, but when it didn't, she just left me to it. Then Mr Hinds, head of discipline, came in with a message for her. He spotted me straight away.

'Stand up,' he said.

And although he didn't name any names, we all knew he meant me. He fixed me with a beady stare. I read somewhere that rodents do that just before they kill their prey. I saw Mr Hinds as a giant rat, whiskers twitching and glassy eyes staring, and I felt sweat trickle down the back of my shirt. My head itched like mad. It is impressively warm inside a genuine Norwegian hand-knitted bobble hat with snowflake design. I suppose on the fjords in Norway you can't take any risks with the cold, but in an art classroom considerably closer to the equator, the heat was excessive. Little beads of sweat leaked down the side of my face.

'Hat, off,' Mr Hinds said.

I stared at him. Please no, not now. Any class but this. Please, not in front of The Goddess.

'Now,' Mr Hinds said. You could tell he was getting a bit peeved with me because he was starting to overheat too. His face had gone all tomatoey.

'Philip,' Miss Franks said, trying to intervene, but Mr Hinds stopped her.

'I am going to count to three and then I want you to take off that ridiculous hat,' he said in a voice that was very final.

Ridiculous, huh? Norwegian knitwear manufacturers would have something to say about that.

'One,' Mr Hinds said, and the entire class put down their pencils and paintbrushes and art stuff to watch. You could practically see the silence ripple round the room.

Everyone's eyes were on me.

If I didn't take the hat off, Mr Hinds would frog-march me to the headmaster and I'd be made to take it off there. And if I *did* take the hat off in class I'd still be marched to the headmaster afterwards. I was in for some serious punishment and humiliation, or some serious humiliation and punishment. It was really just a matter of which order I preferred. If I waited until we got to the headmaster's office, I would spare myself an excruciating scene in front of The Goddess but I would also be buying myself a great big ugly grudge from Mr Hinds. And he didn't get that job as head of discipline for nothing, you know.

'Two,' Mr Hinds said, and someone behind me gasped.

In the end I reckoned it was only a matter of time before I had my humiliating moment with The Goddess. As soon as this hat came off it wouldn't be long before every single, solitary person in the school knew. So I reckoned I had nothing to lose, and just as Mr Hinds got to three I put my hand up and pulled off the hat.

I say pulled it off but actually it felt like I dragged it off in slow motion. The hush of the class and the drama of the moment and my own desperate fear made it seem like it was a scene from a movie where they cut the sound and slow the film right down, just for a minute, just before a big action explosion. I half-expected a motorbike to come crashing through the window and save me, seconds before the hat finally came off.

But my life is not an action movie and a motorbike did not come through the window. Instead the room was filled with gasps and squawks and hoots of laughter. Mr Hinds was apoplectic. His complexion went from tomato to plum in a second. Boy, was I for it!

I didn't dare move but I could see Ang in the corner of my eye. He'd risen from his seat and was moving towards Lucy, who was probably having a right old sneer.

'*Quiet!*' Mr Hinds bellowed and pointed me to the door.

As I left, I turned to see Ang and Holly the Meerkat standing on either side of Lucy. And you know what? She wasn't sneering at me. She was crying.

24

Rules is Rules

The school rang Mum at 11.15 AM and she was in the headmaster's office by noon. My plan had worked: I had forced Mum to leave the house. And, yes, she did still have three layers of disguise piled on her head, but it was a start.

Mum stared at my bald head, dumbstruck.

'I may have no option but to suspend Philip,' the headmaster said. 'It's the rules.'

I think he was just saying that to try to provoke a response from Mum. I mean, what good would suspension do me? It wasn't like my hair would grow back in three days – that's the max I'd ever heard of anyone being suspended. Then I wondered if maybe he meant he was going to suspend me until my hair had grown back. Cool, no school for months. But then I thought, not cool – months of being at home alone with Mum.

'Mrs Wright?' the headmaster said. 'The rules ...'

Mum still didn't say anything. She just stood there like a dumb animal. No offence meant – there are many handsome and majestic dumb animals out there. Only Mum wasn't a bit majestic. It is hard to look anything other than downright silly (not to mention over-dressed) when you are wearing a wig *and* a scarf *and* a hat.

The headmaster sighed and shifted uncomfortably in his seat.

Apparently there is a condition where people become mute for no biological reason. (Yes, I do watch too much TV.) Well, I reckoned Mum had developed the condition. She had not uttered one single sound since she'd come into the headmaster's office. She just kept staring at me with big watery eyes.

For a moment I was terrified. *Please God, NO!* I would drop down dead there and then if she did her *Tyrannosaurus rex* impersonation. I considered falling down on my knees and begging her not to cry but then I realised that her watery eyes weren't empty and desolate like the day before when she was howling at Susie; they were sort of sad *and* happy, and oddly proud-looking, all at the same time.

'I take it you didn't know about this?' the headmaster said, trying to fill the enormous gaping void left by Mum's silence. He was beginning to sound a bit desperate. 'Mrs Wright?'

And then … you will never in a million, in a trillion years guess what happened next, so I am just going to come right out and tell you: *my* mum, the impressively silent Mrs Kathleen Mary Joanna Wright, put her hand to her head and took off her hat. And then her headscarf. And then, her wig.

She reached a hand towards me and the two of us stood there before the headmaster, silent and bald and smiling.

It was the headmaster's turn to be struck dumb. The look on his face was priceless. I wish Ang could have been there to see it.

Miraculously Mum's power of speech returned pretty swiftly after that.

'I have cancer,' she said, plain and simple.

And I know this might sound a bit odd, but I felt really proud of her.

I didn't get detention or suspension or lines or anything. In fact Mum and I got a cup of tea in the school's good china cups in the headmaster's office. They were white with blue Chinesey flowers on them; the kind old ladies drink from. You'd think a headmaster would have something a bit more manly than that, wouldn't you?

Anyway, never mind the teacups; I learnt something else that day. You know how people say 'Good news travels fast'? Well guess what? *Bad* news travels even faster. The news of my bald head and Mum's cancer was all over the school by lunchtime. The headmaster said that I could go home for the rest of the day, but I reckoned the worst that could happen already had.

And then I met The Yeti.

As usual, he was slow on the uptake. I think he hears things through a special filter, like a phone line breaking up so that instead of hearing 'Philip Wright shaved his head because his mum has cancer,' he heard, 'Wright … shaved … head … cancer.' Then he put it all together, in the wrong order.

He walked right up to me, said, 'There's nothing funny

about cancer. You wouldn't like it if someone made fun of your lot.'

And then he punched me in the stomach. Really hard. Really, really hard. I keeled over and started choking like a six-stone weakling. (I really need to bulk up.) Within seconds a crowd had gathered, but instead of shouting 'Fight, fight!' the crowd was solemn and silent.

'Cancer,' somebody whispered, and they all turned and gave The Yeti the evil eye. Even Lucy.

The Yeti got a suspension. Apparently shaving your head trumps punching someone in the guts. There is a lesson to be learned there. I think.

Dear Harry Hill
Don't you just love chaos theory? You know I told you I shaved my head? Well, the knock-on effects were astounding. Mum started going out again, the headmaster gave me a cup of tea, Lucy 'The Goddess' Wells started smiling at me, and my bully got a suspension. Apparently he thought I was making fun of people with cancer, so he punched me. I am now very confused about the big oaf. I hate him for thumping me but I am impressed by his impulse to defend cancer-sufferers everywhere. Ain't life weird.
    Yours sincerely
    Philip Wright

25

Mrs Angry

'Things are going to change around here,' Mum said, brandishing a duster at me.

I didn't like the sound of that. I'd shaved my head to make things go back to the way they were. I didn't want more change. I'd had enough of that already, thank you very much.

But things did change. For starters, Susie moved in. She came around one day with a big box of her stuff.

'It's only temporary,' she said. 'Just until you are on your feet.'

I knew I'd done a remarkable and inspiring thing (thank you) getting Mum out of the house but I wasn't sure I could keep it up and I had a terrible suspicion that we had a long way to go yet, so Susie moving in was great. She got to work on Mum, planning out each week and each day, each hour. Every little bit of Mum's time was mapped out: sleeping, reading, exercise, food. It was really weird, like Mum was learning how to live again.

Once Mum had got some kind of rhythm back (getting up during the day and sleeping at night like a normal non-vampire parent) she had more energy. Unfortunately, she decided to pour her new found energy into being angry. Luckily she was angry about 'things' and not about me but still you had to be careful. If you disagreed with Mum she was liable to bite your head off, and if you agreed with her she was just as likely to bite your head off (apparently for 'just humouring' her).

'There is nothing for cancer patients in this no-horse town,' she said one day over tea. She had her angry voice on again.

'Hmm,' Susie said. (This was her preferred method of dealing with Mum when she was in Angry Mode.)

'Well, I am going to change that,' Mum said, banging her cup down on the table.

'Hmm.' (Susie again)

'It's not good enough. The big towns and cities get all the help and we get what?' She didn't wait for an answer. 'Zilch, nada, *NOTHING*! That's what we get. Well, I'm going to fix that.'

'Hmm,' Susie said again, but this time she creased her forehead and looked sideways, first at Mum, then at me.

'How are you going to do that?' I asked.

'I am going to set up my own cancer help group,' Mum said.

Susie choked on her tea and spluttered a spray of liquid across the kitchen table.

'It's time someone around here did something,' Mum said, getting all fired up. 'I'm going to set up a support group that gives information and help and ...'

'All by yourself?' I asked.

'All by myself,' Mum said. Her face was all flushed red and sort of holy-looking.

Good old Mum. Patron saint of cancer victims.

Honestly? I thought the idea was totally barmy (I really was 'just humouring' her) so there was no need for Susie to shoot me that look which screamed, *Shut up you fool*. I know Susie was worried that Mum would exhaust herself but I didn't really think she should worry too much. Like Mum said, this is a no-horse town; where did she think Mum was going to get all these cancer victims to support? She'd be lucky to find more than one or two.

I was wrong. Apparently one in three people gets cancer. Our house was inundated. I came home from school one Wednesday afternoon to find the living room crowded with women.

'Oops,' I said to Mum. 'Sorry, I didn't know you had visitors.' And then I saw them. Twenty assorted women, all wearing wigs or bandanas, or in Mum's case just sporting a bald noggin.

'Why don't you make us all a nice pot of tea?' Mum said.

What did she think I was? I would've needed an industrial-size teapot and two whole cases of Jaffa Cakes to get round that lot.

'I've got homework to do,' I said and backed out of the room.

I went upstairs and lay down on my bed. This was not the kind of development I had hoped for when I shaved my head. I just wanted things to be normal. I wanted Mum to be normal. I knew she could never 'unhave' cancer, but

I didn't want to have to think about it all the time. It was boring. And depressing.

It wasn't long before I heard a knock at my door. Mum must have made the tea herself because she had a mug for me and an iced bun on a saucer.

'Shop bought,' she said and smiled.

I took the bun and swallowed it in two bites.

'You never wolf down my buns like that,' she said.

'Your buns provide an aerobic workout for the jaw. It takes about twenty minutes to chew through the outer crust.'

'The girls would like to meet you,' she said, dropping all pretence of bun chat.

'No.'

'They've heard all about you.'

'No.'

'They think of you as a hero.'

'No,' I said, but I could feel myself starting to weaken.

'You're something of a celebrity.'

How is a boy supposed to resist the lure of celebrity? I could just see their adoring smiles.

'No,' I said.

But this time Mum knew she'd won.

'I've told them you are a brilliant comedian,' she said. 'And we could do with cheering up. It's pretty heavy going banging on about cancer all afternoon. We need some fun.'

So she wasn't enjoying all this cancer business. That was a relief.

'You're just the man for the job,' she said, rising to go.

'I am,' I said. You cannot argue with the truth.

'You could wear those daft Harry-Hill-lookalike glasses you and Susie bought when I was in hospital.'

'I could,' I said.

'So you'll come down? Just for five minutes?'

'I think it'll take a lot longer than that. I have a load of new material to try out.'

I decided to start with that animal joke about the donkey who walks into a bar and the barman says, 'Why the long face?' They were bound to love that.

I pulled off my Norwegian bobble hat, checked my specs in the mirror and went down stairs to meet 'the girls'. When they saw me they gasped. Mum was right: they did think I was a celebrity. Excellent. I cleared my throat and began.

'Did you hear the one about …'

'Wait,' one of 'the girls' said. (She was about seventy, so calling her a girl really was a bit of a stretch.) 'Wait just one second; I need to get comfy.'

Then she put down her tea cup and took off her wig.

'Ah ha!' someone else said and took her wig off too.

And then the rest of them nodded approval and did the same! And I was surrounded by a room fool of baldies.

'Now we all look a bit like Harry Hill,' I said.

Mum coughed and shot me a disapproving look.

What? What's not to like about Harry Hill?

'He's right, you know, we do,' someone said, and started giggling.

And once she'd started, she couldn't stop. And then the woman beside her joined in and pretty soon they were laughing away like hyenas.

And so, our very own Harry Hill Appreciation Society was born.

Dear Harry Hill

Did you know that a side-effect of chemotherapy is that it makes everyone look like a weird version of you? I know this for a fact because a crowd of Mum's cancer friends have started coming round to our house and when they take their wigs and scarves off, they all look a bit like you. Even the ones who don't wear glasses. So if you ever have chemotherapy you will have nothing to worry about because you will look just like yourself. Isn't that good to know?

I also thought you might like to know that I have got my comic genius back. I have been performing every week for Mum's friends. They think I'm hilarious. Which I am. They call themselves the Harry Hill Appreciation Society (on account of all the bald heads and the jokes) and they are planning a big fundraising bash to raise money to renovate an old camper van and turn it into a mobile cancer help unit for rural areas and no-horse towns like ours.

You will notice that I have written you a longer letter than usual this time and that is because I really need your help. Mum is expecting me to go on stage at this fundraiser bash and entertain the crowd and I was wondering if maybe you could help me out with some new material. The cancer women have heard all my stuff already. Write soon, the fundraiser is in a few weeks. Actually it might be better if you phone; our number is 02881765432.

Yours sincerely
Philip Wright

26
Fairground Attraction

I really loved the whole fundraising, camper-van, cancer-road-trip thing.

One of the girls' husbands donated his ancient campervan (a bit like Scooby Doo's) and somebody else knew somebody who knew a handyman who said he could fix it up for us. Admit it, you have always wanted to live in a camper-van. Think of it: the tiny sink; the miniature fridge that can hold only a pint of milk and one egg; the bed doubling up as table doubling up as car seat. And the freedom to go wherever you want. Except our camper-van couldn't go anywhere on account of it only having three tyres and missing an engine.

We got to keep it in our driveway until it was fixed and I was allowed to go in and mooch around in it any time I wanted. And the best bit was that I sometimes saw Ang looking jealously at the van from across the street. I bet he wished we were best buddies now. Well, tough. He chose The Yeti; I chose 'the girls' and their crazy camper-van project.

There was one big problem with the project – it required money. Everyone gave what they could, but even I knew it would never be enough, so we all sat around thinking up ways of raising money.

After some very uninspired suggestions like a sponsored knitathon (no way) and a sponsored silence (yawn), someone came up with the idea of a 'cancer fun day'. I thought putting the words 'cancer' and 'fun' in the same sentence was not a clever idea, but I was alone in thinking this because everyone else latched on to the idea and said, 'Yes, let's have a fun day!'

What d'ye know!

So we all started talking about how we could hire the parish hall for the day and have lots of games and treats.

'We could have a coconut shy,' someone said.

'And a hoopla.'

'And candy floss.'

'And custard-pie throwing,' I suggested. I pictured The Yeti covered in gloop.

'And a make-your-own-smoothie corner,' said someone else.

'Good idea. And healthy-eating stalls.'

'And unhealthy-eating stalls. Marge here makes a mean cream cake.'

The ideas kept coming. One of 'the girls', it turned out, was a yoga instructor and she offered to give taster lessons.

Another described herself as a 'nail technician'. I thought that meant she manufactured nails and screws for a living but apparently not. She does women's nails and she has some really wacky designs like spiders' webs. 'The girls' all thought it was a great idea, so I went along with it. What do I know about women's nails?

Then one woman who didn't speak very often piped up and said she was an archery expert, and if the weather was fine she could set up some target practice on the lawn outside the hall. Awesome.

There was only one dodgy moment when someone suggested a cancer information desk and some kind of cancer screening booth. This 'girl' had obviously lost the plot. It was supposed to be a *fair*. We were supposed to have *fun*, so I said, 'Wrong time, wrong place. We want people to eat candy floss and throw custard pies at each other, not run screaming from a booth because they've just found out they have cancer.'

There was a terrible silence while everyone stared at me. Then the oldest 'girl' said, 'Ah, the wisdom of youth.'

They all nodded in agreement and went back to talking about sensible things like face-painting and a balloon man for the little kids and a tombola (does anyone even know what a tombola is?) and hiring a DJ.

Then Susie suggested fancy dress. I hate fancy dress. My deep-seated hatred of it stems from that time when Mum sent me to a fancy-dress day at primary school dressed as a school boy. She called it irony. I called it excruciating. I think I must have groaned out loud at the fancy dress idea because Mum caught my eye and gave me one of her looks.

Then she said, 'OK, scrap that Harry Hill fancy-dress idea.'

'Fine,' Susie said, 'It was only a thought.'

'Hang on,' I said. 'Harry Hill?'

And within minutes, with a majority show of hands and a lot of grinning, it was agreed that the fun day would be themed fancy dress – everyone should come dressed as Harry Hill – black suit, big specs, bald head and all. Genius.

And the best bit?

Everyone agreed that, as well as the DJ, we would need some live entertainment; a comic performer to act as compere (that's posh for host), and who better than – *ME!*

Oh My God! I love those girls. This could be my big break.

27
Fever Pitch

Two weeks before the big fundraising bash Mum was rushed into hospital. Luckily Susie was still staying with us because it all happened in a panic in the middle of the night when Mum woke with a raging temperature and couldn't stop throwing up. I stared at her horrified as she vomited into a basin at the side of the bed. I patted her shoulder stupidly a few times because I couldn't think of anything else to do. She winced under my hand. I couldn't tell if she was wincing because I was getting on her nerves or because that slight touch was hurting her; either way, it wasn't good so I stopped.

Susie called the doctor from the bedroom phone and an ambulance came immediately. All they would say was that Mum had a temperature (duh!) and that it was worrying. I thought that was ridiculous because I have had a temperature plenty of times and I have never been rushed into hospital because of it. So it was obvious that they were lying to me.

'They're lying,' I said to Susie. 'You're lying. People don't go to hospital just because they have a temperature.'

'Cancer patients do,' Susie said, trying to calm me down. 'It's just routine.'

'No, it's not. It's not routine. If it was routine it would be in all those cancer leaflets Mum litters the house with. "Week 15: go to hospital with a temperature."'

We were standing outside the hospital ward at the time. They wouldn't let us in because they were 'settling' Mum in. She didn't need them to settle her in; I could've done that. I could have tucked in her sheets and put her stuff in the bedside locker. I could have set out her picture of me sitting on Granda Joe's knee – the one she kept beside her bed at home. That would have settled her. I could have laid out her lipstick and that tiny mirror she carries around in her bag 'for emergencies'. They didn't know how vain Mum was. They didn't know anything about her. They didn't know that she only liked one pillow because she got a crick in her neck if she used two. They didn't know that she takes her tea with just the right amount of milk – the colour of digestives, *not* the colour of shortbread. They didn't know that she likes to sleep in full unspeaking darkness, the kind of darkness that made a little kid stub his toe on the doorpost when he wandered into her room in the middle of the night, needing her.

They didn't know anything.

'What do they know!' I yelled at Susie and thumped the door to the ward with my fist. Really hard; hot pain shot through it.

Susie stepped back, shocked. Then she took my hand and said, 'You're right. This is serious. We just have to wait.'

And then we just stood there gawping at each other like two people who were lost on the moon without a map.

When a nurse finally came to talk to us she said Mum was asleep and shouldn't be disturbed. We'd have to call back tomorrow.

I didn't sleep. Neither did Susie. I could hear her in the spare room, twisting and turning and sighing. At about three in the morning, when the house was still and I assumed Susie was dozing, I slipped out of bed and crept in to Mum's room. I didn't put the light on. The duvet was rumpled up in a big mound, pushed to one side. In the dark you could almost think she was still there.

I sat on the edge of the bed and laid my hand on the mound of duvet.

Then I whispered into the darkness, 'It's all right, Mum. You are going to be all right.'

Aren't you?

Then I got up and wrote to Harry Hill.

Dear Harry Hill

Mum was taken in to hospital because she has a temperature that she can't get rid of and they can't give her the horrible chemotherapy and she looks awful and the doctors won't talk to me because I am too young. So I thought, with your medical background, you might be able to tell me if she is going to be all right? She has a temperature of 40 and is vomiting. Is that normal? Do you think she'll be better in time for the fundraising fair, which is two weeks away?

You can ignore all the stuff in my other letters if you want, but this one is deadly important. Please write back quickly.

Yours sincerely

Philip Wright

PS: Can you die from a temperature?

28

Doctor, Doctor!

When they finally let us in to see Mum the next afternoon, she looked awful. Really awful. Susie burst into tears when she saw her, which was seriously unhelpful. And all I could think of was Granda Joe, which wasn't much help either since he was dead.

Have you ever seen a dead person in real life? Well, not in real life because then they wouldn't be dead, they'd be alive. I mean a dead person in reality, not on the telly. I have. I saw Granda Joe laid out in his coffin when he died. The coffin was open so that you could go in and keep him company if you wanted. Weird, but kind of nice too.

Anyway, I couldn't help thinking of Granda Joe like that because Mum's skin was the same waxy yellow his was when he died, like all the blood had been drained out. I'm not trying to be melodramatic here; I'm just telling you what I saw.

I desperately wanted to give Mum a hug but I couldn't because of all the drips and tubes and things, so I just gave her a little peck on the cheek. Her skin felt cold but it was sticky and there were tiny beads of perspiration on her face. So that is what is meant by a cold sweat. I thought it was just something English teachers made up to explain what a paradox is.

Mum smiled at me and pursed her lips in a kiss but she didn't lift her head from the pillow. She said it felt too heavy. A tonne weight she said. Her voice was all whispery and worn out. Instead, she just reached her hand out to me and I sat there holding it. It was sweaty and cold too.

Susie stood behind me and said nothing but I could tell she was crying even though she was trying to pretend she wasn't. I could hear her breathing catch. None of us had anything to say.

After what seemed like two nano-seconds the nurse came and told us to leave. Mum was tired, she said. I didn't want to go and I must have started making a fuss because Susie had to put her arm around me and pull me away from the bed. I hated myself then because Mum looked really upset.

Then I realised she wasn't upset with me, because she lifted her hand and beckoned me back. I leaned in close and felt her breath on my face. It was warm and weak.

'Tell me a joke,' she said. 'I love you ... telling me jokes.' She stumbled on the words.

I thought a 'Doctor, doctor' one seemed appropriate, so I told her the one about the man who goes in to the doctor with a banana in his ear and a cucumber up his nose.

She was asleep before I got to the end of it.

A nurse coughed and came to check Mum's drip. She pressed some buttons on the monitor and said, 'That's better, Kathleen, isn't it?'

And even though her voice was kind, I hated her. My

mum's name is Kathy. Not Kathleen. No-one calls her Kathleen. No-one but me, when I am making fun and pretending to boss her around.

The nurse turned to me. 'Mum needs to rest,' she said in her soft, sticky voice.

Don't call her Mum, I wanted to yell. *She is not your mum.* But I didn't. I just sat there holding Mum's hand and ignored the nurse.

'It's time to go,' the nurse said, looking to Susie for help.

'Philip?' Susie said.

I ignored her too. What I really wanted to do was climb up on Mum's bed and lie there beside her but the big BOLD-font sign (Times New Roman, point size a million and forty-two) telling relatives *NOT* to lie on the beds put me off.

I will never be a hero. Heroes don't heed signs like that. Heroes just plough on and do something heroic. Not me, I am a very obedient person. Biddable, Granda Joe used to always say.

But just then, I would not be bidden. I would not move. I pulled the chair up close and laid my face on the pillow beside Mum and let her feel my breath on her cheek. She seemed to be barely breathing, like no air was getting in or out because she hadn't the strength to make it.

I moved my head closer, put my lips to her ear and breathed in. And I know it was stupid but I just had to do it. I had to breathe some life into her.

I don't remember leaving the ward or the drive home from the hospital. I don't remember Susie making me cocoa or fixing me a hot water bottle or tucking me into bed like a baby, though she later swore she did.

I do remember lying in my bed thinking of Granda Joe. I saw him stiff in his coffin, yellow and cold. Dead. Not coming back. Not ever.

Mum was that same colour, and almost as still. What if she did not come back? What then? Whose kiss would I duck then, whose soft nagging would I ignore? Who would know to leave my games kit at the front door on PE day because I have 'a head like a sieve'? Who would know that I like my beans on toast *off* the toast, that I like sugar in coffee but not in tea, that I have a slight intolerance to cheese? (It makes me farty.) Who would ruffle my hair (so seriously annoying) and ask, 'How was your day?' and genuinely want to hear the answer?

And even if someone, Susie, anyone, could learn all this, even if Mum could write a guide and leave it – 'An A–Z of Philip Wright' – it would still be all wrong. That person, that 'replacement' would be all wrong. They would feel wrong and smell wrong and move wrong. They would sound wrong and think wrong. They would *breathe* wrong. I could not live in that wrong world. Mum had to come back. She had to.

And so I lay there in the middle of the bed curled up in a ball and I cried out, 'Come back! Come back! Mum, *please come back*!'

Dear Harry Hill

I want you to know that my outlook on life will never be the same again – I'll never be able to admire my heroes again. And it is all your fault.

How could you? You go on TV and are all nice and funny and friendly. You sometimes even have ordinary people on your show. But really, you don't care about ordinary people like me or Mum.

Would one letter have killed you?

This is the last time I will ever write. I've had it with you.

Goodbye

Philip Wright

29

Operation Sneak

Mum came home from hospital two days before the fundraising fair. Susie and I made a real fuss of her and wouldn't let her do anything, not even make a cup of tea.

'I'm fine,' she protested.

But she didn't look fine. She had lost weight and was pale and tired and bald.

'You need to rest and get your strength back,' Susie said.

'You need to eat cakes and lots of fattening food,' I said.

Mum smiled at me and then turned to Susie. 'There isn't time to rest. The fair has to be organised.'

'It's all taken care of,' I said. 'Really, you don't need to worry about a thing. There are loads of activities and my routine is *smooth*. Wanna hear it?'

'Actually,' Susie said, 'I have a job for you. Can you go down to the supermarket and get some of that herbal tea the nurse recommended?'

'But we did the supermarket shop yesterday,' I said.

'I forgot the tea,' Susie said.

'But it's miles away,' I protested.

'One mile.'

'It'll take me ages.' I turned to Mum. 'We can do without

it. Can't we?' I said in my best *poor me* voice.

'Please,' she said in an even better *poor her* voice.

Susie gave me a five-pound note and told me not to hurry back, but I did. I raced into town and into the supermarket, grabbed the tea and raced back. I was out of breath and sweating when I got back but I'd done it in just under half an hour. A personal best.

'Crikey,' Susie said. 'Lightning man.'

But she seemed more annoyed than impressed. She'd come out of the living room when she heard me at the front door and she stood blocking my way in.

'You are going to kill me,' she said, 'but I forgot that we need straws.'

'Straws?'

'Yes, straws. Bendy ones,' Susie said. 'For the drinks tomorrow.'

'But it's raining now,' I said.

'So? People still drink through straws in the rain.' She thrust a twenty-pound note into my hand then she slipped back into the living room.

I went into the kitchen to put the tea away and just as I was closing the cupboard door I saw it – a box of herbal tea. Unopened and identical to the one I'd bought. Either Susie was lying to me or she was developing Alzheimer's. That was all I needed. As if I hadn't enough to do looking after Mum. I went into the hall wondering if I should confront Susie but as I was passing the living-room door I could have sworn I heard a man's voice. I went outside and tried to sneak a peek in the window as I was passing along the street but it was too far away. I did notice a strange and very posh-looking car, though, parked in front of our house. Maybe the two were connected.

When I got back to the house, soaking wet and clutching a bumper batch of straws, the living-room blinds were drawn, and if that wasn't suspicious enough, Susie was waiting for me at the front door and instead of letting me in, she sent me to 'check' on old Mrs Casey. That's when I knew something was definitely up because Susie has never shown any concern for Mrs C's welfare before. I protested but Susie wasn't budging.

Mrs Chihuahua seemed really pleased to see me. I hadn't been expecting that. I don't know why, but it hadn't occurred to me that she might actually enjoy human contact. I thought she preferred animals. Anyway, she offered me a glass of juice and some soggy digestive biscuits and we sat in her back room until Susie called to say it was OK for me to come home. I learnt something new that day: old folk talk about dead people all the time and have very loud ticking clocks.

Back at our house the mysterious posh car had gone, the blinds had been opened and there was no-one in the living room but Mum and Susie, both looking very guilty. They were definitely up to something.

30

The Best Medicine

You know how people sometimes say they nearly wet themselves with anxiety or excitement, just to be funny? Well, I can tell you it is not one bit funny. On the day of the fair my nerves were wrecked and I kept wanting to pee and we ended up arriving late.

Not just because of me – it was Susie's fault really. She was driving, but she kept us all late talking to someone on the phone about something to do with the fair that was 'none of my business'. She seemed to have forgotten that I was the host and the star attraction. And the star attraction's nerves couldn't take much more of this.

And then when we did finally get there Mum refused to be pushed around in a wheelchair, so I had to sit with her instead of getting ready backstage. I don't understand Mum – I have always wanted to break my legs and get spun around in a wheelchair. I thought everyone did. People kept coming up to Mum and hugging her and saying she looked great, which was really kind because she didn't look great; she looked sick. But seeing the place put a smile on her face. *Anyway,* I had to sit there 'minding' her and Mrs Chihuahua, who'd come along in Susie's car. (NB savage smelly Chihuahua, three adults and one boy in a Mini is not a good combo.) Meanwhile Susie dashed around talking to people on her mobile like she was the important one here.

PMA, I told myself – at least we had good seats. We could see everything: the streamers and balloons and fairy lights and pictures of Harry Hill all around the walls; the stalls with food and drink and games and demonstrations; and the *dozens* of Harry Hills. There were so many bald wigs and big black glasses it was difficult to tell who was who, but I definitely saw Ang and his mum and dad over at the coconut shy, and I'm fairly sure I saw Lucy and her meerkat friend Holly having their nails painted by the nail technician woman. There was a crowd of others from school too and they were all in bald wigs. I even saw the headmaster and, unbelievably, Mrs Gray, who came up and said hello and didn't mention poetry once. And she was wearing a bald wig too!

Then I spotted a woman carrying a large camera taking loads of pictures. Mum had said journalists would be coming. Think of it: the Harry Hill Appreciation Society would be in the paper! I'd be famous.

'Do you think they'll have us splashed all over the front page?' I said.

'Maybe they will,' Mum said with a grin.

And then a little kid ran in, squealing something about more cameras and men and I don't know what else, because just at that minute the DJ played a big blast of Harry Hill music which meant I was about to be introduced on stage.

Except I wasn't on stage or backstage or side stage, and before I could get past Mrs Casey and her humongous knitting bag which she'd brought with her 'just in case', the lights went out and the DJ started introducing me.

'Ladies and gentlemen,' he said, 'please put your hands together for our host today.'

I seriously thought I was going to faint or choke or explode or implode or something. (Not sure I know the difference between those last two.) I would look like an idiot when the curtains opened and I wasn't there, except no one would see idiot me, but you know what I mean. This was a disaster. I tried waving frantically at the DJ but he didn't even notice. He just went on doing his introduction. And he was clearly loving it because he kept dragging it out: *Ladies and Gentlemen ... let me introduce ... your host today ...*

And then he cranked the music up some more and the curtains opened. And there on stage was the real – the *actual* – Harry Hill.

The crowd went wild, and I very nearly wet myself.

Luckily, I have exceptional bladder control because the next thing that happened was that Harry Hill (yes, *the* Harry Hill) called me up on stage! I think you'll agree that pee-stained trousers is not a good look on anyone, especially not someone who has been invited on stage with a world-class comedian and who then spent a whole half hour entertaining everyone with a comic routine which *the* Harry Hill described as classic. Do you hear that? I am *classic*.

I played it safe and started with some animal jokes. You can't go wrong with animals. People either love them and think the joke is cute or they hate animals and think it's OK to make fun of them. It's a win–win situation. After that, I moved on to a whole pile of 'Doctor, doctor' jokes, and you know what? Harry Hill knew them all and actually joined in, so that I was the patient and he was the doctor and it was like we'd rehearsed it or something, and we were this brilliant, hilarious double act.

You know how people say you should never meet your heroes, because you'll be disappointed? Well, they are *so* wrong. Harry Hill was even nicer and even funnier in real life, and apart from the 'Doctor, doctor' double act, he hardly interrupted me at all when I was on stage.

After the performance, Harry Hill's 'security people' swooped in around him and announced that he couldn't stay long, but he did sign some autographs (mostly on people's bald wigs), and then he sat down for a chat with Mum. Wasn't that thoughtful? He could see she was still a bit too weak to be standing up in a crush of mad autograph-hunting fans. It's probably his medical training. Or maybe he is just a nice guy because he even had a bit of a chat with old Mrs Casey. He gave Alfred Pickles a pat on the head and said something funny about Paris Hilton and dogs in handbags but it was obvious Mrs Casey hadn't the faintest idea what he was on about. To tell you the truth, I'm still not convinced she even knew who Harry Hill was.

He told Mum I was a credit to her and said that I was really thoughtful, which was nice, because no-one has ever called me thoughtful before. I really wished The Goddess had been there to hear that, but she was across the room gossiping with The Meerkats.

Once we were off stage, I came over all star-struck and could barely say a word to Harry Hill. I had all these questions in my head that I'd stored up for years but I couldn't get any out. I just sort of grunted, but Harry didn't seem to mind; he made a comment about me being shy, and said he had really enjoyed reading all my letters. He'd only got them a few weeks ago – all in one batch.

'They just kept piling up,' he said. 'I spotted them when I went in to the office to sign some documents one day. That's when I got on the phone to your mum.'

He said my letters had really made him laugh, but I couldn't see how that could be the case since they were an impassioned plea for help from a desperate child, not a string of jokes. But I didn't argue. All I could think about was that final awful letter I'd written him. It just goes to show how heroic your heroes are when they can overlook a thing like that.

As he was leaving, Harry Hill kissed Mum on the cheek and she went red, and everyone burst out laughing. After he'd left, people couldn't stop smiling. Especially me and Mum. It was like he had cast a spell on us. In fact the whole place was infected with a party atmosphere and no-one wanted to go home. And just in case there was any danger of that, the DJ got up and told people not to even think about leaving because there was lots more entertainment.

Then he said, 'Wow, ladies and gentlemen, Harry Hill! Can you believe it?' for about the sixtieth time.

'So,' I said to Mum, 'that's what all the secrecy and Susie's "private" phone calls were about.'

I had to hand it to them. They could probably get jobs as spies or something. I could never in a million years have kept a secret that big.

'Group-hug!' Susie squealed, bounding over towards us. And right there in public view she squished Mum and me into her arms.

Now, don't get me wrong, I could forgive nearly anything after arranging that whole Harry Hill surprise, but I did still sneak a look around the hall to see if anyone was watching us. And of course they were. Lucy and Ang and Holly the Meerkat were staring right at us. With stupid big grins on their faces. Ang and Holly still had their bald wigs on, but Lucy was taking hers off and was shaking her golden Goddess hair free. She looked more lovely than ever.

When they saw me looking over, all three started to come towards me. And for the second time that day I thought I was seeing things, only this time the whole thing was in slow motion splendour, like one of those soppy bits in a film.

Ang and Holly were walking slowly towards me.

And they were holding hands!

'You and Holly!' I gasped.

'How could you not know, mate?' Ang said to me. 'How could you not see?'

He turned to Holly and grinned at her like an idiot. The best idiot friend in the world.

I turned to Lucy. 'So, not you and Ang?' I said

'*No!*' she said and shook her incredibly beautiful head and laughed.

'So that just leaves you and Eddie Lyttle.' I felt a bit sick just saying the words.

'Are you mad!' Lucy said. 'That's probably illegal or something. He's my cousin.'

'Cousin?' I squealed, yes, *squealed*. I really must learn to master that impulse to sound like a strangulated mouse. It is *so* not cool.

'Yes. *Cousin*,' Lucy said. 'You'd know that if you ever stopped to listen, but you're too busy hating him. And you shouldn't because you actually have a lot in common.'

Now, I may have resembled a love-struck poodle (a bald one) but I was not about to pretend that I had some kind of bond with The Yeti. I am neither fat, hairy nor brainless.

'Yeah, right,' I said.

'Yes, right,' Lucy said, pointing across the room to where Holly and Ang had gone.

I didn't get it at first. Then I realised they were talking to The Yeti – but he wasn't The Yeti any more. His hideous mane of hair was gone. And it wasn't hidden under a wig. He had shaved off all his hair. Just like me.

'That woman standing behind him with the blue bandana is his mum,' Lucy explained. 'Aunty Claire. She has breast cancer too. Her hair is starting to grow back now and she says she looks like a hedgehog without her bandana, so she kept it on.'

I was speechless. So I just stood there. Speechless.

'Ha!' Lucy said, shaking her incredibly super-gorgeous head. 'Don't tell me the famous I've-swallowed-a-dictionary Philip Wright is lost for words?'

The famous Philip Wright just stood there like a dummy. A very stupid dummy.

And then, as if I wasn't feeling stupid enough, Lucy said, 'Honestly, Philip, you are so wrapped up in yourself, you don't even notice what's in front of your nose. Shall we go over and talk to them?'

If my life were a cheesy, made-for-TV American movie, I'd have said yes; we'd all embrace and The Yeti and I would become best mates and live happily ever after, possibly going in to business together in adulthood as highly successful bald-wig manufacturers.

But I don't live in a TV movie, so I said, 'Not yet. I like it here.'

And Lucy said, 'Me too.'

She nudged me with her elbow and giggled. 'How could you not know that Ang and Holly were barmy about each other?'

I looked at her and shrugged. She stopped giggling and took a step closer to me. 'How can you not see?' she said slowly.

And then – you are so seriously never going to believe this – Lucy slipped her hand into mine. And we stood there holding hands and smiling, like two people who had just found the answer to everything.

Now, I don't want to come over all philosophical and kill the mood, but you know how old people say *Laughter is the best medicine* and you think no it's not, you cannot laugh your way out of a nasty case of athlete's foot? (Trust me, I know.) So, while I knew I wasn't going to actually cure anyone with jokes, the fact is that there were a lot of happy faces at that fair. The members of the Harry Hill Appreciation Society had never looked so good. They were shining with happiness. Even Mum. I hadn't seen her look this good in months. So there must be more than a grain of truth in that whole laughter-is-the-best-medicine thing.

Maybe I'll write to Harry Hill and see what he thinks.

31
A Shining Moment

You'd think having cancer and surviving chemotherapy and undergoing radiotherapy and facing down death and coming out the other side would mean you wouldn't sweat the small stuff any more, wouldn't you? Well, you'd be wrong.

One day, after all Mum's treatment had ended and they'd declared her well enough to go back to work, I came home from school to find her clutching a black velvet dress and crying, *bawling*, into it. Big fat tears ran down her cheeks and splashed on to the velvet. They sat in unburst blobs on the fabric.

I tried desperately to figure out what the dress could symbolise because it was clear to me that no-one, not even Mum, could get that upset over a piece of clothing. But I couldn't figure it out so I just put my arm around her and said, 'Never mind.'

'It doesn't fit me any more,' she blubbed and let out a fresh wail of despair. 'I can't go back to work in a tracksuit.'

You'd think losing a boob would mean Mum would've shed a pound or two, but the opposite was true. Part of the problem was all those drugs they kept giving her. First they gave her drugs that made her vomit all the time. Then they gave her drugs that made her really hungry. All the time. So she went on a diet. Quite a cranky diet, as it happened. Living on lettuce leaves and Cream Crackers does nothing for your mood. She only smiled if the scales said she'd lost weight but the smile only lasted a few minutes, and then she'd be back to shouting at me for waltzing around the house eating all the time. Which was unfair because I don't waltz.

Poor Mum. I really wished she could lose some of that weight because even though I've told her (and so has Susie) that it is a small price to pay for your life and what harm is a few pounds, I know that it matters to her. I know how vain and beautiful she was before all of this started. So in an attempt to help her lose weight, I started keeping my junk food stash in my wardrobe, and together we ate slimmed down portions of lettuce leaves and cucumber, and the see-through diet soup that Mrs Casey brought round. The main ingredients of which seemed to be water and onions. Apparently it had nil calories. It had nil taste either but I ate it anyway, just to keep Mum company.

Apart from poor old Mum and her squidgy tum, which was clearly going to take some time to fix, the rest of my life started to mend remarkably quickly. Ang and me just went back to being Ang and me. We didn't talk about it or think about it, or whinge about it, we just did it.

My girlfriend Lucy (yes, I said *girlfriend*) says that if Ang and I were girls we'd have had to talk it all through and analyse it and make promises and resolutions and say sorry before we could be reconciled. I am *so* glad I am not a girl. It must be exhausting thinking about stuff all the time. I prefer to keep my head empty. Much simpler.

And talking about my head, my hair started to grow back and, much to Mum's relief, so did my grades and things seemed like they were really getting back on track. I even impressed Mrs Gray one day. I had been making Ang laugh, so she moved me to the desk at the front of the class that she keeps for 'dunderheads and ne'er do wells', and that's when this amazing and weird thing happened.

After I'd been moved, Mrs Gray said we were going to do some poetry. I think that instead of announcing it, she should have just ambushed us because as soon as she uttered the word 'poem' the class started talking and chucking scrunched up balls of paper around and tapping their pens and groaning and pulling faces and making gestures like they'd rather kill themselves than read a poem.

Anyway, she started handing out the poem and because I was at the front of the class at her dunderheads' desk, I got a copy of it first. And since I had absolutely no other form of entertainment available to me, I read it. It was about a boy peeling spuds in the kitchen with his mother one Sunday morning when the rest of the family was out at mass and they just worked in silence and their heads were together so that their breath met. It was sort of magical, like a dream. But then in the second verse the boy was a man and his mother was dying and people were praying around her bedside and it was scary until he remembered that time peeling spuds with her. As soon as I read the poem, the weird thing happened: sounds from the classroom fell away, and it was like I was in a time capsule or something, where I could see my younger self – with Mum hanging out washing, and with Granda Joe hammering nails in his shed. It was like watching a movie trailer for my life with the sound turned down. All this from one solitary poem! It was mind-blowing.

'So, folks,' Mrs Gray said, 'in this poem, the poet is writing about his mother, and it's on your end-of-term exam paper, so listen up. Who would like to read?'

You'd think someone of Mrs Gray's professional maturity would know by now that the answer to that question is always no-one.

'No-one?' she said after a desperate look around the bowed heads of the class. 'OK then, I will.'

She started to read the poem aloud and one or two people shut up to listen.

I wish I could remember it all to repeat the words here but I can't and no way am I going to ask Mrs Gray for a copy. I am one of those people who do actually learn from their mistakes. Anyway, when she'd finished reading, Mrs Gray asked us what we thought it was about and nobody answered so she did what teachers always do in those circumstances: she started picking us out one by one.

'Ang?' she said.

'Potatoes?' Ang said hopefully and everyone laughed.

'Matthew? What do you think it's about?'

'Huh?' Matthew Brown said, without lifting his head

from the desk were it was lying as if it was so heavy he needed a rest from carrying it around all day.

Mrs Gray sighed.

'Fiona, what about you?'

'Dunno, Miss,' Fiona said. 'Is it about liking potatoes better than going to church?'

'Philip?' Mrs Gray said in this really defeated voice.

'It's about memory,' I said, 'and love and loss.'

'Oh!' Mrs Gray said, looking startled. 'Go on.'

'It's about a man remembering time spent with his mother when he was a boy. Ordinary special time. When it was just the two of them and they peeled potatoes in silence and loved each other without having to say it. And then when she is dying that memory comes back to him to take care of him and help him. And the memory of his mum shines out, and it is like a moment. A gleaming golden moment. And that is what memories are, aren't they? Because even if someone dies and leaves you, you can never unknow them. You can never unhave them. They are yours for ever and they can come back and help you in your memories when you need them.'

I stopped. There was silence all around the room and everyone was staring at me, including Mrs Gray. Her face was all flushed red and she looked like she was in pain. So I figured I must have got this poem all wrong. 'I think,' I added, as if that would make me look less stupid.

Mrs Gray blinked at me and turned away to wipe the board even though there was nothing written on it. 'Philip, oh, gosh – very good,' she said. 'Very – excellent.'

And even though her voice sounded funny, I think she meant it. 'Excellent' is not a word Mrs Gray likes to over-use.

When she turned back to the class her voice and face were normal again.

'Now,' she said, 'can you all write down two examples of alliteration. That's two Ls and one T.' And that was that. My one very 'excellent' moment in English was over.

32
Yeti Another Day

So there I was, making my way down to art class, when a thick hand landed on my shoulder. Eddie Lyttle. I froze and felt his fingers press into my still-six-stone-weakling frame. I told myself I had nothing to be afraid of, but it didn't work; my breathing started to get all choked up and panicky. It felt like my Adam's apple had swollen to ten times its normal size and was pressing on my windpipe. Not cool. If I choked to death like that, there wouldn't be a court case because Eddie hadn't even done anything. There'd be no forensics, no inquest, no dramatic courtroom ending.

Eddie pressed down harder, then shook me to make me turn, and as I did, he shoved something sharp into my stomach.

'What's wrong with you?' he said.

When I didn't answer he shoved the sharp thing into my stomach again.

'Take that,' he grunted.

Now, I don't care what Lucy says about him being 'nice, really'. He needs to speak more clearly if he wants to make friends. Grunting is very off-putting.

'Go on,' he mumbled, 'take it.'

I looked down and saw that he was shoving a book at me. Interesting murder weapon, that. Death by book. I looked at the cover; it had a picture of leaves and dried fruit on it. Wow. Maybe he was planning to bore me to death.

'It's a book,' he said, shoving the book (hardback, glossy, very pointy corners) into my gut again.

'Wow,' I wanted to say, 'a book-shaped book – who'd've guessed!' But I have turned over a new leaf. My girlfriend Lucy (have I mentioned I have a girlfriend?) says that I can sometimes give the wrong impression and come across as a bit of a smart alec. So I just said, 'A book?'

'Yeah, dummy. A book,' Eddie said. 'Your mum asked my mum if she could borrow it. It's about eating healthy after cancer or losing weight or something.'

And then I really was a dumb-y: The Yeti, Eddie Lyttle, my sworn enemy, was doing something nice for my mum. Not his own mum, *mine*. And, well, what is a six-stone weakling meant to do in the face of such un-bully like behaviour?

'Thanks,' I said. Not quite the articulate and heart rending speech of reconciliation you might have hoped for, but then we are teenage boys (almost), so what do you expect?

And he said, 'No problem, mate.'

Mate? Eddie Lyttle called me 'mate'!

And then he slapped me on the back and trudged off. Leaving me late for art.

Note

The poem referred to in chapter 31 is from a sonnet sequence by Seamus Heaney called 'Clearances', which was voted Ireland's favourite poem of the last one hundred years by RTE radio audiences in 2015. The sonnet has no title, but is referred to by its first line, 'When all the others were away at Mass'. It was first published in *The Haw Lantern* (1987); it also appears in Heaney's *New Selected Poems 1966-1987*; or you can find it online.

About the Author

Christine Hamill lives with her son in Belfast and teaches creative writing in a college of further education. This is her first novel and her first book for children. She is also the author of a non-fiction book for adults, B is for Breast Cancer.